ABOUT THIS BOOK

From this *USA Today* Bestselling Author - For a vila warrior, love only comes with death.

During World War I, vila warrior Jerina Ventus's life irrevocably changed when she saved a wounded soldier's life and helped him return to his hometown in Colorado. Twenty-five years later, she's restless and longing for another adventure beyond her forest. Little does she know, her sister Kosa will deliver the opportunity to her.

Thane Beltaine grew up hearing stories about the beautiful and fierce immortal warrior who saved his father's life. When Jerina's sister Kosa shows up in his hometown on the arm of a wicked mage, Thane volunteers to find Jerina and bring her back. He never expected to meet the woman who was more legend than real and definitely didn't think they would clash about every little thing.

Jerina's temper and patience are tested as they travel to Colorado to rescue her sister, who at first seems reluctant to be saved. She needs to outsmart the mage and find a way to release Kosa from his control, and she needs Thane's help to do this.

Reluctantly, they work together to save Kosa, and an unexpected love begins to grow. But vila are cursed to never find true love—if they do, he will quickly die a gruesome death.

LEGENDS OF HAVENWOOD FALLS BOOKS

Also try the main Havenwood Falls series; the YA line, Havenwood Falls High; the darker, sexier side of town, Havenwood Falls Sin & Silk; and the local supernatural college, Sun & Moon Academy.

Stay up to date at www.HavenwoodFalls.com

ALSO BY CHAR WEBSTER

GIFTED SERIES

Discovery, Book One

Exploration, Book Two

Transformation, Book Three

Acceptance, Book Four

Experiments, A Gifted Series Prequel

MYSTIC UNIVERSE: STOLEN MAGIC, BOOK ONCE OF THE MYSTIC MAGIC SERIES

Forgotten Magic, Book One of the Mystic Darkness Series

HAVENWOOD FALLS

Changing Fate, Havenwood Falls Legends Book 13

Saving Tannor, Havenwood Falls Holiday Anthology

CHANGING FATE

CHAR WEBSTER

To Briella
Love is worth fighting for.

CHAPTER 1

Obnoxious laughter followed Jerina's ungraceful and rapid descent to the ground from the thick branch she had been perched upon. With a wave of her hands, gusts of wind pushed up against her free fall, slowing her plummet to a slight drop and landing her lightly on her feet.

Her sister, Kosa, was still cackling like a hyena when Jerina stalked over to her. Scooping up a handful of snow, she dumped it on Kosa's blond head in retribution for the snow blast her sister sent to knock her out of the tree. The icy shower coated her soft leather handmade jacket.

Kosa shook the snow from her long straight hair. "I've never caught you unaware! You should have seen your face when you fell."

Jerina growled at Kosa. "You should be patrolling, not messing around!"

The sisters faced each other with the same graceful height, same lithe build, and same long blond hair. Even though there were a few years separating them, they could nearly pass for twins.

"My shift is finished. You would know that if you hadn't been pouting in that tree!" Kosa prepared herself for Jerina to attack. This was a fight that had been brewing for years.

Jerina swung out with her fist, but Kosa ducked out of the way while thrusting her leg out to trip her sister.

The girls ended up in a tangle of long arms and legs as they rolled across the forest floor, kicking up snow and leaves in their fury. They ignored the fierce growl that continued to gain in volume but were pulled apart when sharp teeth sank into the soft leather of Jerina's left boot.

"Damn it, Rela! If you tear my boots, I'm going to send you off to the next country!" Jerina yelled at the regal mountain lion that was still growling and showing lethal fangs. Rela was not intimidated in the least by her outburst. The mountain lion shook her head while still grasping Jerina's brown suede boot, making sure the girls knew she wasn't going to let go until they stopped fighting.

Jerina raised her hands, and wind started to whip through the trees, blowing the mountain lion's fur, but she stood firm. Sighing dramatically, Jerina released Kosa and fell back onto the forest floor, breathing heavily.

Rela dropped the boot with what sounded like a snort, but she stood close to the sisters, making sure they didn't continue to brawl.

Kosa ruffled the velvety tan fur of their good friend. "You could have waited a little longer before interrupting us."

Jerina glared at her sister. "Why are you picking a fight today, Kos?"

"You have not been yourself for years, not since you returned from your trip, but lately it's become far more severe. What is the matter?" Kosa wasn't the only one to notice the change in Jerina. Their mother had begun to ask questions, and that was never good.

Rela's head was leaning over Jerina's shoulder as she sat up, so she pushed it out of the way. It sounded like Rela was laughing at her. She was about to reply that nothing was wrong but decided to speak the truth. "I find myself restless."

"You've always been content here in our forest." Kosa was the one who would seek adventure whenever possible.

Rela settled down on some soft moss, not minding the patches of snow, and closed her eyes, ignoring them since they had stopped fighting.

"I love it, but . . ."

"You need something more," Kosa finished for her.

"Yes!" Jerina whipped her hands up, creating a cyclone of leaves, sticks, snow, and wind around the three of them. "I feel as if I should be doing something, but I do not know what."

"We could venture into town and find some humans to have fun with." Kosa had been sneaking off to town whenever she could, but she didn't want her sister to know how often.

Jerina narrowed her gaze. "What have you done?"

"We are not speaking about me. We are discussing your melancholy mood." Kosa was not going to let Jerina intimidate her.

"You know we cannot become attached to humans."

Kosa rolled her eyes. "We cannot get involved with anyone." Kosa spread her hands out wide, and the cyclone stopped. Everything rained down to the ground in a flurry of debris. "No one is around to hear us. You don't need to draw unwanted attention to this area."

"Kosa, I've seen the little gifts that are left for you."

Kosa's eyes grew round, but she smoothed her shock away and tried to act casual. "I have happened upon a few trinkets. They don't mean anything. They could have been left for anyone."

Jerina raised an eyebrow. "Who is he?"

Kosa had no idea how the conversation shifted to Jerina interrogating her. "I don't have any idea what you're talking about."

"Kos."

"Maybe you should go back and visit Tannor."

"Your attempt at diverting the conversation will not work. Tell me about him." Jerina didn't like the dreamy look in her sister's eyes. She also didn't want to talk about Tannor and her trip across the world. She felt drawn to Colorado but not romantically. She had developed a friendship with Tannor, and that was it. No deeper feelings were involved. Tannor loved his wife more than anything, and Jerina had helped him get back to her when he had been seriously injured.

"There is nothing to say." Kosa began to bounce in place, something she did when she was nervous and not being entirely truthful. She forced herself to stop and face Jerina. "I'd rather talk about you and why you have become insufferable lately."

Jerina thrust her hands toward her sister, and hurricane force winds blasted Kosa back several feet before Kosa diverted the gust upward. Jerina's glare would have scared some of the warrior trainees.

"Do not trifle with me." She stopped the wind when Rela roared.

Kosa cracked her neck back and forth. "You have been horrid to everyone, and you have been drifting off alone whenever you're not on duty."

Jerina sank down onto a fallen tree trunk. Her first reaction was to argue, but her sister's tone stopped her. "You should not exaggerate."

"Mother has noticed." Kosa had told their mother that some of the newer trainees had been goofing off instead of working hard, and that was the reason for Jerina's moodiness. It had only been half of the truth, but it had satisfied her.

Jerina pulled a stick from the log and picked at its bark. "I've been feeling a pull toward Colorado. I do not know why it's so strong after all these years."

Kosa sat down next to Jerina.

"I've been longing to travel." She knew it was the wrong thing to say as soon as it came out of her mouth.

"Tell me about the gifts and the man." Jerina narrowed her eyes at Kosa.

Kosa growled silently, cursing her big mouth. "You cannot let anyone know about this."

"Tell me at once." Jerina knew that a man had been leaving little things for her sister, but those gifts had become more frequent and more elaborate.

Kosa took a deep breath. It was time to explain everything to

Jerina. Out of all the vila warriors, her sister was the only one who went out into the world and returned. Others had left, but only to find tragedy and heartache. Men were the downfall of the vila.

"I've been watching the humans in town. They fascinate me."

Jerina inhaled quickly. "Were you seen?"

"Not at first, but then I found a note pinned to the tree I take shelter behind."

"What did it say?" Jerina stood and began to pace the small clearing, scanning the area for anyone who might be listening to their conversation.

Kosa sighed wistfully. "It said, 'I thought only angels had the power to stop a man's heart.'"

Jerina rolled her eyes. "He was trying to charm you with pretty words."

"It was sweet." Kosa sighed again. "The next day, a white camellia was tied to the tree with another note. This one said, 'My destiny is in your hands.'"

"That sounds ominous." Jerina was starting to get worried. Something didn't feel right.

Kosa laughed. "That is what the flower means."

Jerina frowned at her. "How do you know that?"

Kosa picked up a stick and began to twirl it through her fingers. "I read the books in the village library."

Education was extremely important to the vila. Even though most never ventured into the world, all the women were required to master many subjects and numerous languages.

"I don't understand your obsession with books." Jerina had been more interested in world history, government relationships, politics, and the world wars that had been plaguing their forest.

"You have not read anything for pleasure. I would not care for books either if all I ever read about was warfare." Kosa could talk about this topic forever.

"I wish to hear more about him." Jerina always had to get her sister to focus on one topic at a time. "What happened next?"

Kosa groaned. "A few days later, he left me a gold silk scarf softer than a rabbit fur. This time the note said, 'No flower as delicate, no scarf as silken, no earthly creature as ethereal.'"

"Have you spoken to him?" Jerina couldn't believe her sister had been fooled by gifts and pretty words.

Kosa pulled a gold chain from under her tunic and twirled the star that was dangling from the chain. "Yes. Two days ago, I found this star necklace with another note. 'It is not in the stars to hold our destiny but in ourselves.'"

Jerina raised an eyebrow and frowned, not commenting.

"It's a quote from William Shakespeare." Kosa sighed. "I spun around, scanning the area, only to find luminous golden eyes focused on me. He nervously shifted from foot to foot and ran his hands through his sandy-colored hair. He was waiting for me to find his gift. We talked for hours."

"You can't be that foolish. Kosa, you didn't tell him who you are, did you?" Jerina's anger was making the wind whip around the trees. Rela roared her displeasure.

"Jerina! Stop! He's sweet and kind, and he loves nature." Kosa twirled around with her arms out. "I'm going to see him tonight. Come with me. You can meet him and see how wonderful he is."

Jerina grabbed Kosa's shoulders with both hands. "You are acting like you are in love. You must remember the vila curse!"

As vila warriors, Jerina and Kosa were sworn to protect their vila sisters and their forest. As descendants of wood nymphs and fae, the vila were volatile magical women who shunned men and society.

"I am not in love with him." *Yet*, Kosa thought. "I am having fun and *living* life. We are so isolated here. I want to see the world and experience what it is like to mingle with humans and other supernaturals. Travel, like you did. He said he would take me anywhere I want to go."

Jerina wiped her hands down her face and tried to calm her raging emotions. "You don't know him. He could be dangerous!" She was shouting and couldn't seem to stop.

"I knew you would react this way! That is why I didn't tell you!"

Rela growled loudly and moved to stand between the girls.

Jerina ran her hand across Rela's fur, trying to calm herself. Kosa was always too trusting.

"Please do not see him anymore." Jerina rubbed her temples. Vila hardly ever became ill, but their conversation was causing her head to ache. "If you want to leave here for a while, I will take you away."

"I knew you wanted to leave here, too. You should visit Tannor and his family." Kosa needed her sister to focus on something else.

"I've already told you that I don't remember where he lives. He told me that I wouldn't remember, but I didn't believe him. Everything is clear up to the train station in Colorado and from leaving on the train to come home. I have a vague recollection of a small town, but that's it."

"Then that is the perfect reason to go back there." Kosa crossed her fingers.

Jerina grasped the idea. "If I take you there, will you promise me you won't see that man again?" Jerina pressed. "It will only end in heartache for you. If he is your true love, he will die, and you will never be the same. You cannot risk your heart like that. Remember we're immortal."

Kosa kicked the dirt and uncrossed her fingers. Jerina never gave up on something once she set her mind on it. Her shoulders slumped. She didn't want to end her romance, but she knew it was probably for the best. "I need to tell him goodbye."

Even though Kosa had said what Jerina wanted to hear, her entire body filled with dread as she watched her sister disappear from view.

CHAPTER 2

"*J*erina! Jerina!"

Dropping down from her perch on a boulder looking out over the valley, Jerina landed in front of the novice warrior. "What's happened?"

The girl looked terrified, shifting from foot to foot. "Kosa is gone!"

"What do you mean, gone?" Jerina started jogging toward their village. The girl needed to run to keep up with her.

"I saw her get into a vehicle with a man!" The girl didn't follow Jerina into her house. Novices had to be invited inside their superiors' homes.

Jerina cursed. "I'm going to wallop her!"

She went directly to her weapons cabinet, pulling out several knives and sheaths. Jerina needed to be fully armed when she went hunting for her sister.

A storm had been brewing for three days, the same amount of time that Jerina had gone without any sign of her sister. She was going to have to tell the vila elders that Kosa was gone. She dreaded that conversation with their mother.

Jerina had been searching for Kosa for two weeks. At first, it had been a series of near misses, but it seemed as if something was keeping Kosa just out of reach. The Second World War had also made things difficult for Jerina. Traveling was more challenging and everyone was secretive with the German army everywhere around.

Jerina had tracked them through Poland, but had lost them. There hadn't been a sign of Kosa or her companion for the last few days. She was losing hope.

As leader of the vila warriors, she couldn't abandon her responsibilities. The vila were sworn to protect their forest and all who resided in it.

Her training duties and patrols could not be missed. When the vila had too much free time, they became bored and their more mischievous and malicious tendencies came out. Jerina needed to make sure her warriors focused their energies on strengthening their skills instead of causing trouble with humans. The elders had forbidden the vila from mingling with humans and revealing their secrets. Times had been changing too much, and magic was no longer something the humans believed in. Their secrets needed to be protected.

Jerina had been scheduling double shifts for all her warriors due to the increased war activity and fighting in the area. The vila had been successful at keeping soldiers from staying too long in their forest, but the war was all around them.

Twenty-five years before, Jerina and Kosa had stumbled upon two soldiers during the First World War. One of the soldiers was shot while saving squirrels and his selfless act caused Jerina to attempt to heal him. When that didn't work because the man had been fae and was shot with an iron bullet, Jerina vowed to help him return home to a mysterious town in Colorado.

Jerina smiled. She hadn't thought of the soldier Tannor in a while.

Pulling her sword from the leather sheath strapped to her back, she prepared to make a sweep of the area with her warriors. A flash of light and a disturbance in the air signaled the beginning of a portal. A supernatural was invading her forest.

Two young warriors circled the intruder. He quickly pulled a matched pair of short swords from inside his coat and parried the warriors' attacks. Jerina noticed that he was simply defending himself, not attacking. His moves were fluid, smoothly arcing the swords back and forth, dueling with the warriors.

Vila warriors were usually tall, five feet eight or more, but the man had several inches on the two warriors. Jerina guessed he was about six feet two. His muscles rippled across his back as he moved his swords, stretching his shirt across his shoulders.

Jerina had to admire his skill and energy. She should end the battle and rid her forest of the intruder, but she found herself mesmerized by him. Even though they were moving too quickly for Jerina to see his features clearly, she felt a familiarity from him. She needed to know more.

One of her warriors stumbled on a branch that the other vila had kicked up and was sliced across her arm by the man. She dropped back from the fight, clutching her wound. Jerina swore she heard him apologize to the warrior.

Before Jerina could engage in the fight, the man expediently disarmed the remaining warrior, flinging the sword into the air and catching it. He faced the two defeated warriors and bowed, swords out to the sides in a sweeping gesture.

Jerina stalked toward the tall, lithe man with golden brown hair, her sword ready to defend her warriors and her forest. The man sheathed his swords and drove the one he had claimed from the vila into the ground.

She stopped before reaching him, stunned at his display. She wasn't sure what to do next. Was he toying with them or was he trying to lead her into underestimating him?

"I've put my weapons away. Won't you?" The man sounded playful in a situation that should have been tense.

"Stop where you are!" Jerina called.

Jerina nodded to a warrior that was in the tree above the man. The vila tossed a net from above, covering him. Jerina approached quickly, placing the tip of her sword at the back of his neck. She nodded to her warriors to move away from her capture.

"Turn around slowly." Jerina poised to take him out if he made any kind of aggressive move, but he seemed much too relaxed to be a threat.

He took his time turning toward her.

"Is this slow enough for you? Have you gotten a good enough look?" he mocked, his hands in the pockets of his long coat.

She was tempted to prick him with her sword. He was dressed as a human, but most supernaturals dressed to fit into society. When he faced her, she dropped her sword with a gasp.

"Tannor?" Jerina motioned to her warriors. "Leave us." With confused expressions and backwards glances, they left the area.

When he realized that she wasn't going to run him through with her sword, he pulled the netting off him and tossed it aside.

The man tipped his head and appraised her, his cerulean eyes twinkling. "No. Tannor's my father. My name is Thane." He continued his survey, absorbing every detail. "You look exactly the way he described you, Jerina."

Jerina counted the time since she had seen Tannor. It had been more than twenty-five years. The baby that Tannor had been rushing home to meet was standing before her as an attractive and arrogant man. He may have been a man, but he was certainly not human. He radiated magic and power. If she remembered correctly, he would be half Seelie and half elf. "What are you doing here? We could have killed you! Why did you engage my warriors?"

Raising an eyebrow, he took his time answering. He couldn't believe he was standing before the famed vila warrior. "Your warriors attacked me first. I could have knocked them both out, but you should have been able to tell that I didn't want to hurt either one of them." His eyes drifted over her once more. "And I'm here because my father sent me with a message."

That got her attention. "What message?"

Jerina wanted to knock the smirk from his face. His father, Tannor, had not been that smug. She ignored his comment about beating her warriors. They would have to train harder. Both had newly completed their apprenticeships. Maybe they needed additional instruction.

"He said to tell you that Kosa was seen in town."

Jerina rushed him with her sword drawn, bringing it just under his chin. "You'd better tell me everything you know right now."

Thane hadn't reacted to her outburst or to the sword pressing into his skin. He was fairly confident that he could hold his own against her. His father had warned him of her temperament, but also of her amazing compassion. He knew that Jerina wouldn't hurt him. Well, he hoped she wouldn't hurt him badly.

"I can't explain it to you here. You're going to have to come with me."

"How do I know you're not lying?" Jerina wanted to believe him, but she didn't know the man before her.

Thane winked at her. "You'll have to trust me."

Jerina pressed the blade a little bit more, but not enough to draw blood. Yet. "Where did you see her, and who was she with?"

"I can't tell you. You have to see it for yourself." Thane shrugged one shoulder. He wasn't in a hurry.

Leaves began to swirl around them. Jerina clenched her fists, remembering that Tannor couldn't speak of his hometown. It was magically protected.

"Are you sure it was my sister?" She pulled the sword away and dropped her arm.

"Yes. He was positive it was Kosa." He needed her to come with him. His father had been concerned about whom Kosa was with.

Jerina wanted to rush off and get her sister, but she had responsibilities. It was troubling that Kosa had ended up in the town that seemed to be plaguing her thoughts for months. "You got here through a portal. If I go with you, can we use that to travel back?"

Maybe the trip wouldn't take very long.

Thane leaned against a tree, waiting for her to make the correct decision to accompany him home. "We can get close, but we can't breach the protective barrier."

Jerina nodded absently, mentally planning all the things she had to do before she left her warriors.

"Are you going to keep pointing that at me?" Thane motioned with his chin.

She hadn't realized she was aiming the sword at him again. Jerina slipped it behind her back and into its leather sheath. If Jerina stuck him, she might get blood on her sword and then she would have to spend time cleaning and polishing it.

"I need to get a few things before we can leave. I also need to put someone in charge until I return." Jerina started to jog toward her house.

Thane began to follow after her, but stopped when she swung around to face him.

"You need to stay here. You can't come into our village. Men are not allowed."

Thane raised an eyebrow, but moved closer to a tree and leaned on it with his arms folded across his muscular chest. "Should I get comfortable?"

Jerina didn't answer. She continued on her way, trying to ignore the eyes she felt trailing her until the path curved from view.

CHAPTER 3

"*W*e're going to be a couple of miles from town. I left a car there so we don't have to walk in." Thane muttered a few words and waved his hand. A shimmering portal opened in the air between a couple of trees.

Jerina shifted her small leather bag higher on her shoulder and followed Thane, pausing only slightly to examine the flickering disturbance. She had never traveled by portal before, but she knew a few of the vila elders had used them.

Thane stepped into the portal but turned once on the other side, waiting for her to step through.

Jerina hesitated, suddenly feeling as if her life was about to change once again.

"Are you coming?" Thane called.

With a groan, she stepped through to a wooded area along a quiet mountain road. She saw Thane head toward a cream-colored vehicle with large black tires with white rings along the silver wheels. He told her they were called white wall tires. Jerina wondered where the top of the vehicle was.

"Isn't she swell?" Thane asked, running his hand over the polished fender.

"She?" Jerina glanced around, looking for a female.

Thane grinned. "My car."

"You call your car a she?" Jerina frowned at him.

Thane shrugged, but pulled open the door for Jerina to slip inside. "It's a Delahaye 135 convertible."

She sank into the soft red leather seats and ran her hand over the matching dashboard. The last car she had been in was so different from this one. Nowhere near as luxurious. Glancing behind her, she was surprised that there was not another bench for sitting.

Jerina considered him, confused by his reference to the car. Shaking her head, she asked, "Are we going?"

Thane started the vehicle with a roar and pulled out onto the road. Jerina loved the way her hair blew out from behind her as the car moved faster. She could get used to traveling like this. The wind was a little cold on her face, but it was thrilling.

The view was amazing and somewhat familiar. She had loved the snow-covered mountains before. They surrounded the valley on all sides, protecting the town and hiding it away from the world. It reminded her a little of her mountains in Poland.

After several moments, Jerina felt a pressure building around them and a sudden intense headache. Her skin tingled and itched from the cascade of magic drowning her as they crossed the barrier. Jerina grabbed her head with both hands and tried to breathe deeply to get past the pain.

Thane slowed the car to a stop and turned toward her, concerned. "Are you feeling poorly?" He reached out and cupped her cheek. "Supernaturals don't usually react that strongly to the wards." He brought his hands up to her temples and began to massage slow circles.

She didn't say anything, just concentrated on breathing. When the ache started to recede, she leaned away from him.

Thane smirked as he wiggled his fingers. "I knew that would make you feel better."

Jerina glared at him, turning to face the front of the vehicle with her hands fisted. One minute he was being nice and then he had to open his mouth.

Thane chuckled and put the car in drive once more. They drove for a few minutes through the woods and passed by a stone sign with big, bold metal letters. "Welcome to Havenwood Falls, Jerina."

Her head began to ache again, but differently. Flashes of things and bits of memories scattered through her mind, but nothing fit together. She blinked a few times to clear her head, but the partial scenes continued to swirl.

Thane watched Jerina closely. "The memories from your time here before will come back. Sometimes they come back all at once, but with others, it might only be pieces. Don't try to focus on the memories too much. It will only make your head hurt more."

Jerina nodded and rested her head against the seat. She wasn't used to the rush of magic she felt from this town. It was much stronger here than in her forest. "Are you taking me to Kosa?"

"No. We're stopping at my parents' house first." He continued quickly when she looked like she was going to argue. "They made me promise I would bring you there before we do anything."

"Aspen." Jerina smiled slightly. "Your mother's name is Aspen."

Thane nodded. "Yes. Your memories are returning already. It usually takes a little longer."

They drove through a quaint town with Victorian-style homes and huge shady trees that lined the road on both sides. Jerina was happy when Thane slowed down so she could absorb everything they drove past.

She remembered a little bit of the town square, but didn't recollect the majestic gazebo in the center. It was someplace she would like to explore more. The ice cream shop had her sitting up on her seat. She knew that she had been there before and hoped to return once again.

"I had ice cream there!" Jerina pointed to the Charms Soda Shoppe.

"Their sundaes are keen." Thane watched her wide-eyed excitement with amusement.

Jerina's forehead crinkled, not understanding.

Thane gave her a lopsided grin. "The sundaes are really good."

After a couple of quick turns, they stopped in front of a large cottage with a wraparound porch. A swing and several hanging plants decorated the front of the house.

Thane hopped out of the vehicle and approached her side. She remained in her seat with her hand on the door handle.

"I didn't think vila were afraid of anything." Thane opened her door, but she stood and pushed by him.

She frowned when she heard his mocking chuckle. Her response was cut off by the front door opening and a couple walking outside.

"Jerina!" Aspen called as she hurried to the steps and down the walkway. "It's so good to see you!" A tall woman with dark brown hair wrapped her thin arms around Jerina and hugged her tightly.

Jerina pulled back. "Hello, Aspen."

A brilliant smile lit her face. "You remember me?"

"A little. My memories are coming back in pieces." Jerina glanced toward the porch and saw Tannor standing next to Thane. They looked amazingly similar.

Jerina knew that Tannor and Aspen were nearly immortal, so she hadn't expected them to look different, but it was still a slight shock.

Their clothes were the most different. Aspen had on an A-line dress that reached below her knees with buttons running down the length. It was in a dark blue color with tiny flowers printed on it. Tannor was in navy trousers and a light blue button-down shirt. He had his sleeves rolled up.

Tannor bounded down the stairs and scooped Jerina up in a tight embrace. "I'm happy to see you. Please come inside."

They all filtered into the house and took seats in the living room that was just off the foyer to the left. Jerina scanned the inside of the house, trying to remember it from the last time she had visited, but nothing triggered any memories.

Thane watched his parents and Jerina speak excitedly with each other, catching up on many things that had happened over the years since Jerina had last been in town. He had heard the stories before, but he was intrigued to hear about them from Jerina.

"I'm sorry your forest has soldiers in it again." Tannor put his arm across the back of his chair. "At least you didn't have to bring a wounded officer home to his pregnant wife."

Jerina smiled. "I was happy to help you return to Aspen."

Jerina had witnessed Tannor return a couple of baby squirrels to their nest and get shot when World War I had entered her forest. She had been moved by his selfless act and tried to heal him, only his fae nature had prevented him from fully recovering from the iron bullet.

Aspen put her hand on her husband's knee and addressed her son. "If it wasn't for Jerina, we wouldn't have your father with us. I'm so thankful for her."

Tannorsmoothed his wife's hair. "Jerina spent Christmas with us and even saved the Caroling in the Square that year. A strong storm had rolled in, and she blew it over the mountains so we could continue the night."

Jerina laughed. "I had forgotten about that."

Thane loved watching how happy his parents were with each other. He wanted to have a relationship like theirs someday.

Their stories turned to things that had happened during their time apart. Thane was chagrined that many of the stories featured some of his more embarrassing antics.

Aspen excused herself for a few moments and returned with tea and pastries that she set on the coffee table.

Tannor sat forward with his forearms on his knees. "Jerina, I'm thrilled you're here in Havenwood Falls, but I know you aren't here for pleasure."

Jerina leaned back in her seat and gave Tannor her attention. "Kosa disappeared a few weeks ago. She had been receiving gifts from a man and spent time with him. I thought I had talked her into ending their acquaintance, but she ran off with him instead."

Tannor clasped his hands in front of him. "Kosa is with Perun. Do you remember him from your time here? He was the mage from the Green Coven whom you met at the Christmas Caroling in the Square."

"The leech who leered at me?" Jerina tried to remember Perun clearly, but she was only getting images.

Aspen tried to stifle a laugh. "He's the one I told you not to kill, because it would have turned the snow red."

Thane had been quietly listening up until then. "You were going to kill Perun? I would have liked to see that."

He had seen the trouble Perun caused, knowing he would never be punished for any of it. That was part of the reason Thane honed his fighting skills. He wanted to protect his family and Havenwood Falls.

Jerina scrunched her nose. "How would he and Kosa end up together?"

Tannor frowned and rubbed the back of his neck. "I have a suspicion, but I'm not sure."

"What is this suspicion?"

Aspen gave her husband an encouraging nod.

"When you left, Perun asked dozens of questions about you and the vila. He was especially interested in where we met." Tannor rubbed his neck again, but continued quickly when Jerina opened her mouth to speak. "I would never betray you, Jerina."

Jerina smiled kindly. "I know you would not." She began to fidget with the leather string on the top of her knee boots. "Why was he so interested in me? We keep to ourselves."

Tannor rubbed the back of his neck, massaging the tension that was building there. "Not much is known about the vila. That makes some people want to discover more. I think Perun was intrigued by your strength and power."

Jerina frowned at him. "Wasn't Perun a mage?"

Thane leaned against the wall next to the fireplace. "He's not a strong one. He has always wanted more power and a higher status in the Green Coven. Ada is currently the head of the Green Coven, but Perun has always wanted the position."

Jerina scrunched up her nose, not making the connection. "I do not understand what that has to do with Kosa or me."

Thane chuckled. "He needs more power to control the coven. Only the strongest lead them. Perun has ambition, but not the magic he needs."

Jerina turned white, and her eyes grew into large saucers.

Aspen moved next to Jerina and patted her arm. "I don't think he would hurt her. He can be charming when he wants to be."

Jerina didn't want to say her thoughts out loud for fear they might be true. "Would you please excuse me for a moment?"

Without waiting for them to answer, she fled to the front porch.

He wants more magic and power. He couldn't know. It's not something many people know about. Closing her eyes, she prayed that Perun hadn't discovered their weakness. *This could be worse than I thought.*

Aspen stepped outside. "What's the matter, Jerina?"

Jerina whipped around, startled. She usually didn't get caught unaware. "I'm worried about Kosa."

"Let's go back inside and get ready to leave. I'm sure Tannor and Thane would love to walk us into town so we can meet with the Court of the Sun and the Moon. All supernaturals must register with the Court within twenty-four hours of coming to Havenwood Falls," Aspen reminded her. "We should take care of that matter before we do anything else."

Jerina nodded, a few more memories flooding back. "I had to wear a medallion the last time I was here."

Aspen motioned toward the door. "They don't use those anymore. Now they give visitors a temporary tattoo infused with a little magic." Aspen pulled the collar of her dress away from her neck and pushed her hair back. "It doesn't have to be large, just something small. They usually mean something to the person wearing it. Since I'm a resident, mine is permanent."

Jerina leaned closer and saw a delicate flower with a butterfly perched on the top of it. "Do I get to choose my design?"

Aspen nodded. "Yes. Do you know what you would select?"

Jerina thought for a moment. "A snowflake with wind around it."

Jerina stepped inside and stopped abruptly when she heard Thane's voice.

"After all the stories about how fierce she was and how

powerful, I'm not very impressed. I walked right into her forest and took down two of her warriors. I probably could have slung her over my shoulder and carted her back here." Thane's back was toward the door, so she didn't think he had seen her walk inside the house.

Tannor watched his son fly through the air and land in a heap on the floor against the wall across the room. Jerina stood over him with her sword pressed into his neck once again.

"You need some new moves. You've already tried this one out," Thane mocked, seemingly unconcerned.

Tannor moved closer. "Let him up."

Jerina glanced over her shoulder at Aspen and Tannor. Neither of them seemed too worried about their son. She took a step back, but decided not to sheath her sword yet. "I don't have time for your games. I need to find my sister."

Aspen nudged Tannor with her shoulder. "Jerina, we know you want to find Kosa, but you need to be a little patient. First, we need to get you registered and settled."

Jerina scrunched her forehead. "Settled? I can't stay. I have duties at home."

Aspen approached her carefully. Jerina had raised her sword absently. "You can't barge into the Green Coven and demand your sister. Doing it that way will not end well."

"What do you suggest?" Jerina didn't want to waste time, but she also didn't want to scare her sister into leaving town.

"We can walk to the town square, take care of business, and come back here to form a plan." Tannor knew that Jerina wouldn't want to wait.

Jerina slid her sword back in place and started for the door, but Aspen stopped her. "You might want to change clothes so that you don't stick out in town."

Jerina glanced down at her soft leather pants tucked into her worn boots. Both were handmade by one of the vila novices and probably not what human women wore. They probably didn't have leather vests and swords strapped to their backs either. Jerina used to wear long dresses, but since her trip to Havenwood Falls the last time, she had adopted wearing pants.

"Thank you, Aspen. I hadn't thought about my appearance." Jerina walked over to the coffee table and picked up a magazine. She flipped through a few pages until she opened to a young woman in a navy-blue dress that buttoned up the front and reached mid-calf. She loved the open collar, puffed shoulders and three-quarter sleeves.

With a snap of her fingers, she was wearing the dress, along with low kitten heels and a wide-brimmed hat. She even turned her leather bag into the same dark blue clutch purse the model had.

"How is this?" Jerina caught Thane's appraising stare, but he quickly looked away.

Jerina wanted to bring her sword, but didn't think a back holster would be appropriate for town. She twirled it in her hand, and it shrunk down to fit into her purse.

"You look spiffy!" Aspen beamed. "Let me get my hat and handbag, and we can be on our way."

CHAPTER 4

*T*he walk to the town square was uncomfortable and tense. Aspen and Tannor stayed in front of Jerina and Thane. The couple linked arms and whispered quietly to each other every few minutes.

Thane and Jerina kept a few feet between each other in painful silence. Neither would back down from their stubbornness. Aspen acted as their tour guide, pointing out things as they passed. Some of it Jerina recognized, but most of it was new. Things had changed so much since she had been there last.

The courthouse was the same as she remembered and so was the way they had to enter the Court of the Sun and the Moon. The front doors of City Hall were for the humans; the rear door that led down to the basement was for the supernaturals. That was the door they used.

Sheriff Ric Kasun greeted them before they could pass the threshold. "Come in. I want to speak with you before you meet with Saundra."

He stepped aside, allowing them entrance, but stood stiffly, his muscles tense and ready to act.

Aspen and Tannor shared a glance, but didn't say anything. Thane passed the group and flopped down in a seat next to the door.

Sheriff Kasun didn't even glance at Thane. He focused on Jerina. "I'm warning you, I will not stand for any kind of trouble from you. I have already been warned that you are here to force your sister to return home with you. I will not tolerate kidnapping or coercion."

"Pardon?" Jerina couldn't believe what she was hearing. "She is *my* sister and a vila warrior under my command!"

"You're not in your forest any longer. This is Havenwood Falls. We have our own governing body and our own laws. You either abide by them or you will be escorted out of here."

Papers on the desk began to blow across the room, and Aspen's hair lifted from her shoulders.

Sheriff Kasun's gaze narrowed. "Do you want to leave now?"

Tannor stepped next to Jerina, placing a hand on her shoulder and nudging her. "Jerina was caught off guard. She won't cause any trouble."

Jerina's chest heaved. She wanted to blast the sheriff into the next state. She opened her mouth, but Tannor squeezed her shoulder to get her to stop.

"Well?" Sheriff Kasun asked.

"No. I'm not going anywhere without my sister. I'll follow your laws."

He gave her a skeptical look. "I'm not convinced."

"Neither am I," a voice from the hallway called.

Jerina saw an elegant woman in a dark business suit glide into the room. Her hair was tinged with silver streaks that made her look distinguished and polished, not aging. This was a powerful woman. Jerina remembered a little bit about her from her visit before, but not much.

"Hello, Jerina. It's been quite some time. I don't know if you remember me. I'm Saundra Beaumont." She stuck her hand out for Jerina to shake.

Jerina stared at the hand in front of her for a few seconds, before reluctantly clasping it. "My memory is returning in pieces, but I do remember you a little."

Saundra raised an eyebrow. "Good. Then you will remember that I don't play around."

Saundra's hair lifted momentarily, but Jerina managed to make it stop before she got herself kicked out. "Neither do I."

Exhaling with distaste, Saundra moved closer to Jerina. "We don't know you very well, and we don't trust you yet. Your sister is staying with a resident of town and has not caused any trouble since her arrival. She expressed a fear of you."

Jerina made a strangled sound, but Saundra continued.

"We do not get involved in family squabbles unless it becomes a danger to Havenwood Falls."

Jerina folded her arms across her chest, seething and afraid to respond. The only thing she could think to do would be to send everyone flailing away from her with a burst of wind.

Tannor moved closer. "I can vouch for her."

Sheriff Kasun shook his head. "She needs an escort while in town. I don't have a deputy to spare right now. We are short-staffed."

Jerina's face turned red, and her fists clenched. She was having difficulty controlling her emotions. "I don't need an escort."

Saundra eyed her. "Unfortunately, that is the only way you can stay in town."

"No."

Jerina was ready to argue more, but surprisingly, Thane stood up. "I can babysit the vila while she's here."

Aspen's eyes lit up. "I think that is a brilliant idea!"

"Absolutely not!" Jerina would rather spend time with the sheriff and all his deputies.

"Are you sure you want to take on this responsibility?" Saundra asked Thane.

Yawning and stretching his arms out in what appeared to be boredom, Thane shrugged one shoulder.

Saundra took that as confirmation. "It's settled. Jerina will not be permitted to remain in town without Thane being at her side." She faced an irate Jerina. "If you disregard our dictate, you will be banned from town."

~

Jerina was in a daze. Somehow, she managed to keep her mouth closed long enough for her temporary tattoo to be placed on her shoulder and for Aspen and Tannor to suggest that she stay at Whisper Falls Inn since it was closer to Thane's house. Saundra and Sheriff Kasun both agreed to the location. Jerina thought they liked the idea of more people watching her.

Thane held the door for Jerina to step out into the afternoon sunshine. She turned her face up to the warmth and soaked in the renewing energy. She had no idea how she had ended up in such a mess, and now she had to spend time with an arrogant ass.

Thane grasped her elbow to lead her toward a tall Victorian mansion on the corner facing town square. "Come on. I'll take you to Whisper Falls Inn."

Jerina could only nod from the numbness spreading through her body.

They strolled past the gazebo and the couples who were taking advantage of its shade. She wondered if she would ever be as carefree as they appeared to be.

Thane noticed her eyes watching the people meander around the square and the longing look in Jerina's eyes. "Are you too tired to continue on to the inn? We can rest, if you require it."

Jerina kicked him in the shin and stomped toward their destination. She was drawn to the inn's gingerbread trim and majestic turrets. It reminded her of the castles in the books Kosa would read. That thought made her feel sick. Her sister didn't want to see her and was afraid of her?

"Jerina?" Thane's mocking tone had changed to concern.

"We should continue."

As soon as the stepped onto the wraparound porch, the door opened, and a man and woman stepped outside. They moved so smoothly that Jerina could tell that they were otherworldly, but wasn't sure which type of supernatural they were. Their grace and poise showed in their every motion.

Thane smiled at the couple. "Good day to you, Mihail, Irina. I've brought you a guest. This is Jerina Ventus. She will be staying with us for a few days."

Thane enjoyed spending time with the Petrans. Mihail had helped Thane develop his fighting skills and taught him how to win against supernaturals with superior speed.

"Jerina, this is Mihail and Irina Petran. They own Whisper Falls Inn."

Jerina recovered her manners and greeted the couple.

Mihail reached out to shake her hand. "Saundra called to let us know you would be arriving. It's a pleasure to meet you. I hope you enjoy your stay here with us."

He shared a glance with Thane that Jerina couldn't interpret, but she dismissed it. There had been too many weird things happening for her to worry about another odd look. "It's nice meeting you."

Irina reached out toward Jerina. "I'll show you to your room." She scanned the area. "Do you have any luggage?"

Jerina knew that it must look odd to be traveling without a suitcase. "No. I didn't bring much with me."

Irina smiled caringly, her gray-green eyes sparkling. "It's all right. I have a few things that past guests have left behind. We can also walk into town to one of the shops to get some things you might need."

Jerina felt comfortable for the first time since arriving at Havenwood Falls. "Thank you."

Thane called after them. "I'll be back for dinner!"

Jerina could hear his laughter all the way inside.

Irina patted her hand. "Things are not always as they seem. Don't let first impressions guide you down the wrong path."

Jerina scrunched her nose. "I don't understand."

"I know you don't now, but you will. Havenwood Falls is a magical place. Remember that." Irina stopped before closing Jerina inside her room. "We serve dinner at six. Madam Luiza does not like tardy guests."

"I'll make sure that I arrive early. I appreciate your kindness."

Jerina paced around her spacious room, not focusing on any of the elegant but comfortable furnishings. She was restless and basically on house arrest for the next hour before Thane would return for dinner. She didn't know how she was going to deal with him being around her so much.

Jerina flopped down on the soft bed and ran her hand over the cover. She had never slept on anything so fluffy. The bed she had at home was more functional and stiff than anything.

She glanced at the pale yellow flowers on the wallpaper and bedcoverings, which gave the room a springtime feel. "Ughhh," she groaned.

She couldn't go anywhere without Thane, but maybe she could explore the inn. Jerina followed the aroma of freshly baked bread and found a woman with dark brown hair cutting vegetables at a large wood table that looked well-used.

"Hello, Jerina. I'm Madame Luiza."

"Uhh, hi. I uh . . ."

"There is a huge pile of potatoes that need peeling."

Relieved at having something to do, Jerina hurried to the sink to wash her hands and get to work. "I didn't mean to be a bother."

"I'm happy for the company."

Jerina smiled as she picked up her first potato.

They chatted about the town and the tourist attractions that everyone should see while visiting. She didn't remember having a nicer time working.

Thane hurried back to his parents' home. He needed to speak with his father before meeting Jerina for dinner.

He jogged up the street, jumped over the white picket fence, and leaped onto the porch. Tannor was waiting for him in a wicker chair.

"Are the Petrans looking after her?" Tannor asked.

Thane laughed. "I don't think anyone needs to look after her."

Tannor leaned back and stretched his long legs in front of him.

"She's a fierce warrior, but she's also been completely sheltered her entire life. I remember how wide-eyed she was when she experienced everything for the first time."

Thane took a seat next to his father. "You're worried about her?"

"Yes. I'm afraid that she will relinquish her freedom to join her sister." Tannor rubbed the back of his head. "She's going to give you a hard time."

Thane grinned. "I'm looking forward to it." He lost his smile when his father scowled at him.

"If Perun gets control of them both, we are all in danger. There could be no stopping him." Tannor sat up and stared at his son.

"I'm not going to let Perun get Jerina, and I will save Kosa." Thane stood from his chair. "I need to change for dinner. I'll stop by later."

"You're covered in flour." Thane popped his head inside the kitchen.

"I see you left her here in a hurry. Were you afraid I would get you to help too?" Madame Luiza teased.

"No, ma'am. I had a few things to do before dinner."

Jerina noticed how good he looked in his dark gray pinstriped suit with a matching vest. Her dress was covered in flour and a few wet spots.

Madam Luiza walked over to her. "Shoo. Go get ready for dinner. I'm sure Thane will help with setting the dining room.

Thane sighed, and Jerina hurried off to her room. She still didn't have any changes of clothes with her, so she had to use magic again. Surprisingly, she had to concentrate on her magic for it to come forth. She wondered if the tattoo was hindering the flow. Dismissing that thought, she busied herself with fixing her appearance.

Ten minutes later, Jerina jogged down the stairs toward the dining room but almost stumbled on the last step. She hadn't realized Thane was waiting at the bottom for her. She stopped when she noticed his approving appraisal.

Thane inclined his head and held out his arm for her. "Truce?"

She wasn't sure what to do, so she hesitated.

He took her pause as a rejection of his peace offering. "Or not."

He dropped his arm and spun around. Jerina hastily caught up with him and linked her arm around his. He stiffened at first, but then relaxed and smiled down at her.

"You look lovely." He winked at her when her eyes grew large.

"Tha-thank you," she stumbled, not expecting the compliment. Jerina wanted to keep up the conversation, so she searched for a safe topic. "Did Madame Luiza ask for your assistance?"

He chuckled. "Of course she did." He turned a corner and led her into the dining room. "It wasn't too bad. She let me snitch a cookie from the oven."

"I have a feeling it isn't the first time that's happened."

Thane grinned devilishly. "I can't help it if women want to give me treats."

He harnessed his best manners and pulled out her chair for her and then circled the small table to sit across from her. He selected a table by the windows, away from the rest of the room. He wanted a little privacy with her.

Jerina wasn't used to formal dining, so she sat quietly with her hands in her lap. They usually sat around a fire in the center of the village back home. They had houses now, but they still held on to past traditions.

Madame Luiza stopped by her place at the table. "Don't you worry yourself. We're not fancy around here. Just enjoy the food you helped me make."

She glanced around at the other guests, but no one seemed to be paying attention to her. She sighed with relief.

Thane was waiting for more sparks from Jerina. She didn't seem to be the shy type of woman, so her quietness was worrisome. He twirled the wine in his glass. It was a particularly flavorful vintage from the Stone Falls Winery.

"You're staring at me like you're waiting for something to

happen." Jerina dug into her mashed potatoes. They were creamy and buttery and delicious.

"I am. You're too quiet and reserved. It's like a volcano just waiting to erupt or the calm before the hurricane."

She tilted her head and studied him. "I could create a hurricane."

"Madame Luiza would be upset if you interrupted dinner." Thane liked teasing her. Her cheeks turned pink, and her eyes brightened. It was a good look for her. "Have you ever made a hurricane?"

She shook her head. "No, but I caused a massive blizzard when I was young. It's still spoken about."

"How much snow?"

She grinned. "About forty inches. I threw a bit of a tantrum, and the elders had difficulty trying to put a stop to it."

Thane gazed at her quizzically. "Don't all vila have power over the weather?"

"Yes, but some are stronger than others." Jerina didn't want to seem like she was bragging, but she had more control and power over the weather than all the other vila.

"You are the strongest." It was a statement. He could tell by her confidence.

Jerina shrugged with a small smile and took a sip of the red wine. She hadn't noticed that Thane had poured it for her. Jerina scanned the room over the rim of her glass. No one was looking her way, so she felt comfortable to be more herself. With a sparkle in her eye, she dug into her baked chicken and roasted vegetables.

"Do you like the wine?" Thane asked.

"Yes. It's different from what we have back home, but I like the mild taste." Jerina was used to heavier wines.

"It's from the Blackstones' winery. They have been making wine for a very long time here in Havenwood Falls." Thane hoped to take her on a tour of the town and would be sure to stop there.

"Would you like to take a walk around the square? It's a beautiful night," Thane asked when dinner was finished. He was shocked to have enjoyed himself as much as he had. "You don't need a coat."

Jerina glanced around the lobby of the inn, trying to decide. She had nothing to do except return to her empty room. Normally, she could patrol or train with some of her warriors, but those were not options. Thane had been charming all through dinner, so she didn't mind continuing the evening in his company. "Yes. I would love to see how much things have changed since the last time I was here."

CHAPTER 5

*T*hane draped his coat over her shoulders. He offered his arm to her, and this time, she accepted without a second thought.

As soon as they stepped off the porch, Jerina tipped her head up to look at the sky. She waved her hand, and the clouds cleared so that they could see the stars.

"That's a handy trick." Thane loved stargazing. His mother had taught him about the constellations and the stories people had created about them. It was always something he enjoyed.

Changing the clouds had been easy for Jerina. She wasn't sure why her other magic was sluggish, but at least she could still change the weather without any problems. "It can be. Some vila use their powers to toy with humans or to destroy things. They rage against their lot in life."

Thane led her to the gazebo so they could people-watch and continue their conversation. He wanted to hear anything she was willing to tell him. He didn't know much about vila. No one did.

"Many people are not happy with their life, but they don't lash out." Thane sat on the bench inside the gazebo and stretched his legs out in front of him.

Lots of people were strolling around the square, mingling and enjoying the night. Jerina took everything in, learning about the world once again. "Vila are different. All vila are women."

Thane interrupted. "Well, that explains it."

She caught on to his sarcasm. "Funny. There are no men in our lives or in our village."

"None?"

"No. There are none. Anyway, some are born vila, like Kosa and me, but some are created."

That got Thane's attention. "Created? Are you saying they are made? And how are vila born without men?"

"Vila might not live with men or settle down with a male, but that doesn't stop them from taking pleasure when it suits." Jerina knew she shouldn't have brought up men. There were some things she didn't want to discuss with him or anyone.

"That's interesting. So, whenever the mood strikes, you pick the first man you see?" Thane wiggled his eyebrows.

"No. Not talking about that." Jerina groaned. He was not going to let that go.

Thane wanted to ask her more about men, but he was afraid she would shut down and not be so open with him. He felt an uncontrollable need to know more. "Continue. The vila select the first man that piques their interest and then have little baby vila." He paused in thought. "What happens to any boys born?"

"Vila only have girls."

"Hmmm."

Jerina rolled her eyes. "Other vila are not born and grow through life. Young women who are killed while engaged or before they are married sometimes have the choice to be turned into a vila or to cross over to the afterlife. Some of them select becoming a vila for revenge."

"That's a scary thought." Thane could imagine the damage a scorned woman could create. "None of the vila ever want to settle down with a man? Don't any of you want to have a family?"

Jerina knew these questions were coming and prepared to answer him, but another couple entered the gazebo.

The woman's blond head was leaning on the man's shoulder while his arm was around her back, holding her close. Their heads were so close together, she couldn't see their faces.

Jerina wondered what that would feel like, then quickly dismissed the thought. It was too dangerous. Thane stiffened next to her, setting her on alert. She scanned the area for danger, but didn't see any. He seemed to be staring at the couple that just joined them.

Thane took her hand and pulled her to her feet. He hadn't expected this to happen and wasn't prepared for the fallout. He only prayed that not too much damage would occur and that Jerina wouldn't break Havenwood Falls' laws by revealing her magic.

He knew the moment Jerina discovered the identity of the couple before them. The clouds began to gather in the sky, and a distant thunder roared. Thane squeezed her hand to try to keep her calm.

"Kosa!" Jerina shouted. "What are you doing? Why are you here? With him?"

Kosa's eyes became saucers as she faced her sister, but she didn't speak.

"Why, Jerina, how lovely to see you," Perun crooned. He tightened his hold on Kosa, who stood just a couple of inches shorter than him.

"Sister, have you nothing to say?" Jerina couldn't believe Kosa was simply standing there mute.

Kosa lifted beseeching eyes to Perun, but didn't answer Jerina. His light brown hair blew in the breeze Jerina was creating.

Thunder grew closer and louder. Jerina switched her heated stare to Perun. His hazel eyes were filled with malice. "What have you done to her?"

Perun sneered. "You'd better watch yourself, vila. Too many weather changes will cause the humans to wonder what is happening. You wouldn't want to get yourself banned from town."

As Jerina's rage intensified, so did the weather. Thane grabbed both of her shoulders and turned her toward him. "Do you want to save your sister?" Thane glanced to Perun. "I'll get her out of here so you can enjoy your night."

Perun snickered. "Babysitting duty? There are ways of controlling her. Let me know if she gives you any trouble, and I'll let you in on the secret."

Jerina threw her hands toward Perun, but Thane encircled her with a shield, cutting her off from everything.

"I'd advise you to continue your night elsewhere, my friend. She's volatile tonight," Thane called out as he struggled to contain Jerina's magic.

He wished he could open a portal to whisk her away from there, but there were too many humans around. He knew that as soon as he released her, power would explode from her. Thane hoped he could calm her down before that happened. The Court of the Sun and the Moon would have a difficult time containing something like that.

Perun led Kosa away, laughing loudly and watching Jerina with calculating eyes.

Thane began to shake slightly from the force of magic she was pushing outward. The skies had settled, but he knew a torrential storm would rage once she was fully unleashed. He stepped close to her, nearly touching. He bent his head toward her so that he could whisper in her ear. He didn't want anyone to overhear.

"If you wield your power here, you will never save your sister. They will ban you from this town, and she will be lost to you forever. Perun will make sure you never get to her."

Jerina's eyes were blazing fire, and Thane didn't know if he was getting through to her. "You need to calm down so I can release you. I can't do that until I know you won't lose control. I can feel your powers pulsating."

She took a deep breath, and he could feel her power lessen.

"That's it. I can't help you and hold your powers back at the same time." Thane's tone was soft and soothing, much like someone speaking to something wild and untamed.

"He's controlling her!" Jerina shouted. She couldn't get her emotions under control. She had thought her sister was acting out over a man she wanted to be with. Jerina never considered that her sister would be under his complete control.

"Yes. But you can't do anything about that until you let the power go." Thane hoped he could get her to listen to him.

Jerina closed her eyes and centered her power, drawing it into herself. Even though the jerk was going to turn her into the sheriff, she knew he was right. She couldn't save her sister if she was kicked out.

Several deep breaths later, she opened her eyes and focused on Thane. "Are you going to turn me in now?"

Thane pulled back some of his shield to test her. He felt her power withdraw, but he knew she could throw it back out instantaneously. "No."

"How can I trust you?"

"You don't have a choice. You have to trust someone." Thane wanted to earn her trust, but they didn't have time.

Jerina shook her head, wanting to deny him. Her power was starting to build again, so she forced it back. She hadn't had this kind of trouble since she was a teen, many years ago.

"I know you don't think so, but I'm here to help you. Just give me the opportunity to explain everything." Thane ran a hand through his hair. "Please."

Jerina exhaled and dropped her power completely. "I'll listen."

"This would be considered a bribe," Jerina mumbled as she stuffed another heaping spoonful of ice cream sundae into her mouth. A dribble of chocolate syrup escaped and slid down her chin.

"Is it working?" Thane was too interested in watching her devour her dessert to pay any attention to his own. He was glad he remembered his dad mentioning that Jerina loved ice cream. The Charms Soda Shoppe was the perfect place to take her.

Jerina glanced up from her treat to see Thane staring at her. Embarrassed, she wiped her mouth and chin and tried to eat a little more politely. "You're watching me eat. Stop."

"I can't. It's cute. I don't remember ever being that excited about food before." Thane leaned over the table, getting closer to her. They were sitting in a corner booth, facing the front of the shop. Jerina had walked up and down every aisle in the place before they were seated. She loved all of the tourist gifts and pharmaceuticals that she didn't have at home.

Jerina shrugged. "We don't have ice cream or candy at home."

Thane's eyebrows shot up. "You don't have dessert?"

"We do, but nothing like this. Mostly a type of flat cake or tarts." Jerina finished her sundae and contemplated licking the bowl but figured that might be pushing things.

"Want to finish our walk?" Thane asked, sliding his unfinished sundae away from him.

"I want some answers."

Thane chuckled. "I'm going to give you some. I thought you might be in a better listening mood after this." He stood and offered her his hand.

"So, it *was* a bribe."

"I never said it wasn't." Thane walked her around the town square and toward Whisper Falls Inn. He knew they could spend time on the back porch without too many people milling about.

Traffic was getting lighter, and many people had returned home, so they didn't have to stop to greet anyone on their way back to the inn. He was not in the mood to share her with anyone.

Jerina spotted the large wooden swing that was covered with soft pillows. She flopped down, causing it to flow backward before swinging forward again.

"No porch swings at home either?" Thane found himself eager to see what she would enjoy next.

Jerina dropped her foot to stop her momentum. "No. But some

of the younger girls have swings to play with before they start their warrior training."

Thane sat next to her and pushed them forward to start the motion again.

"Why are you being nice to me now? You haven't been most of the day." Jerina needed to understand this complicated man.

"What, my charm hasn't been up to your standards?" Thane laughed, but stopped abruptly. Deputy Conall Kasun, Sheriff Kasun's son, stepped out of the darkness and onto the walkway leading to the back porch.

"You need to go inside for the night. You can't leave the inn. The Petrans will watch you until I come back tomorrow." Thane stood and pulled her roughly to her feet.

Jerina had no idea what had just happened. One minute he was being sweet, and the next he was rudely ordering her around. Folding her arms across her chest, she stood her ground when Thane tried to guide her inside. She stomped her foot down hard on his toe and spun around to leave the porch. She froze in place when she noticed they had company.

"Is everything okay, Thane? I was checking up on our new guest." Conall moved into the porch light, but didn't climb the steps.

Thane plastered on a fake smile. "Hello, Conall. Thanks for stopping by. I was just saying farewell."

Conall swung his attention to the vila. "You need to stay here at the inn and not wander around by yourself."

Jerina growled low. She was getting really tired of everyone thinking she was a criminal. "I'm not a *dog*."

She knew he was a wolf shifter and couldn't resist the dig.

Conall stepped closer. "What did you say?"

Jerina smiled sweetly. "I said, I'm not *alone*. There are many people who watch over me."

Conall narrowed his gaze at her.

"I'll walk Jerina inside," Thane called over his shoulder as he tried to usher her away as quickly as he could. "You're asking for trouble."

Jerina shrugged his arm away from her. "Why do you care?"

Before he could answer, Irina joined them, carrying a pile of clothes. "Oh good, Jerina, you're here. I was going to put these inside your room." She turned to Thane. "You can run along."

Jerina was happy to escape Thane, so she quickly hurried after Irina.

CHAPTER 6

*J*erina punched her pillow once again. There was no way she could get comfortable or possibly sleep. She had too much on her mind.

Irina had been so nice to bring her all those clothes. She couldn't believe people would leave so many things behind when they stayed at the inn. Jerina could tell that the innkeeper was trying to distract her from her dark thoughts by rattling on about the town and its many inhabitants.

At first, Jerina wasn't sure which type of supernatural Irina and Mihail were, but she quickly determined that they were some sort of vampire. They were nothing like the bloodthirsty ones Jerina had encountered back home.

The nice woman had squeezed her shoulder and whispered low. "Give Thane an opportunity to speak with you tomorrow. Things won't seem so bad then."

Jerina had her doubts, but she refused to be rude to the kind woman. Irina had given her silky pajamas.

Coffee was not something Jerina had at home, but she had remembered it from before and couldn't wait to try it again. Since sleep had eluded her the night before, Jerina knew she would need gallons of the stuff to keep her awake.

She managed to stumble down the stairs to the dining room and sink into a seat. She was immediately poured some coffee, which she gulped, only to spit out the scorching liquid. She scanned the room to see if anyone had seen; luckily no one had.

Jerina waved her hand over the wet brown stains that were spreading across the white table linen. She watched as the stains dried and disappeared. She was thankful for her father's fae heritage that gave her extra abilities.

"Don't worry about the cloth, dear."

Jerina jumped in her seat, a guilty expression on her face. "You gave me a fright, Madame Luiza!"

The older woman winked at her and flitted away to check on her other guests.

With her breakfast finished, Jerina contemplated exploring the town a little, but knew too many people were watching her. Someone would report her lack of an escort, and she would be kicked out of town.

Groaning loudly, she stomped toward the porch. At least she could spend time outside while she waited for Thane to arrive. If he showed up. They left things unsettled between them, so she had no inkling if he was coming. Jerina hated being at the mercy of anyone.

The tulips and daffodils in the garden drew her attention as they swayed in the light breeze. She felt herself leave the porch and approach the colorful display. It seemed to be reeling her in and capturing her in its beauty. She knelt on the early spring grass by the carefully sculpted flowerbed, running her hands along the petals.

Glancing around to make sure no one was watching, Jerina infused the flowers with a little magic to help them grow. Smiling at her handiwork, she took a few steps backward and bumped into a solid chest. Yelping, she jumped forward, turning quickly to see who had snuck up on her.

"If you want to brush up against me, I suggest turning around first. It's much more fun that way." Perun's leering gaze made her skin crawl.

"What are you doing here, and where is my sister?" Jerina could feel her emotions churning, but she knew she had to keep it together.

Perun continued to undress her with his sleazy eyes. "Would you like me to take you to her? Simply say the words." Perun pulled a tarnished gold pocket watch with a long gold link chain from his vest and ran his thumb over the glass front. "I would never deny the company of sisters."

"You're revolting." The way he fondled that watch made Jerina shiver with disgust. She could feel the dark magic oozing from the timepiece.

Perun stepped forward, attempting to grab her arm. Jerina saw a flash of silver from a small pocket knife clutched in his other hand.

"If I didn't know better, Perun, I would think you were bothering one of my guests, but I know you would never do that. Would you?" Madame Luiza moved around the side of the azalea bush to join them.

Jerina hurried over to Madame Luiza and sighed in relief. She was afraid to even imagine what Perun would have done. Madame Luiza had just saved her.

"Luiza," Perun spit out through clenched teeth. He spun around and marched off the property.

"You need to be more careful," Madame Luiza said, patting her shoulder.

"You have perfect timing." Jerina turned in a circle to make sure Perun had left.

Madame Luiza guided her toward the porch. "Thane will be here shortly. Don't wander around without him."

Jerina flopped down on a wicker chair with an unladylike grunt. She was used to leading warriors and training. She hated taking orders and following directions.

What felt like hours later, Thane jogged up the sidewalk toward her. "I heard you had a visitor this morning."

Jerina shot to her feet and arched a brow. "You heard already?"

"I would have been here earlier, but I had visitors too."

Jerina shrugged, not interested in his visitors or his life.

"Why don't we go somewhere a little more private?" Thane offered his hand.

Jerina shook her head, ignoring his outstretched fingers. "That's not a good idea."

"Sure it is." He leaned closer to her. "There are too many busybodies around here."

She shrugged. "So?"

He leaned even closer and whispered, "A few members of the Green Coven stopped by for a chat. Seems like they wanted to keep me occupied so that Perun could get to you."

Jerina was intrigued. "Let's go."

Thane grinned and led her from the porch and around the back of the inn. Making sure no one was watching, he opened a portal and pulled her through.

Jerina hadn't been expecting him to do that, so she stumbled but righted herself quickly. "I thought you couldn't open portals through the town wards."

"We are still inside of them. I figured it was the quickest way to get somewhere private, and I thought you might like to see the falls." Thane watched her closely as she spun around to gape at the rushing water.

"Wow! I can feel the magic of this place. It's exhilarating!" Jerina held her arms out to her sides and soaked in the feel of the magic.

Thane grinned. He knew it was a good place to bring her. "You like it here?"

She twirled with her arms out. "I love it."

Thane slid a backpack off his shoulder and removed a blanket, spreading it on a flat-topped rock. "Here. We can sit and . . ."

"And you'll explain everything?" she challenged.

He grinned wickedly. "Yes."

Jerina settled on the blanket, folding her legs under her. "Why are you being nice today?"

Thane ran his hand through his hair. "I never wanted to be rude to you. I had to be."

Jerina started to rise, but he placed his hand on her arm to stop her.

"Give me a chance to explain," he pleaded.

She leaned back, folding her arms in front of her. "Go on."

"Perun has been setting things up for a long time now, convincing people that he is an upstanding citizen. He's been donating to the town, helping with things that need doing, and taking care of problems. The Court likes having him around. He doesn't mind bending or breaking the rules for them."

"What does that have to do with you?" Jerina was happy for the information on Perun, but she wasn't making the connection to Thane.

"My family loves this town and will do anything to protect it. I grew up learning magic, defense, and weaponry so that I could protect my family and Havenwood Falls. I help out Sheriff Kasun and the Court."

"Great. So, you brought me here for a lecture. Save it." Jerina slid off the rock and stomped to the edge of the water.

He followed after her. "No. I'm trying to explain everything to you. Please listen for a few more minutes."

She nodded, twisting around to face him.

"My dad has been watching Perun for a while, suspecting that he was up to no good with his obsession with vila. We knew he had been making trips all over Europe looking for you and your people. He wants your power."

"We're not so easy to find." Jerina kicked at a small stone with the toe of her boot. She was thankful Irina had provided a pair of sturdy pants, boots and a lightweight jacket. She knew most women didn't wear pants often, but she preferred them.

"No, you're not. He searched for twenty-five years."

"Until he found my sister."

"Yes. When my dad saw Perun in the town square with Kosa, he knew something wasn't right. He had approached them to say hello to Kosa, but Perun wouldn't let her speak. When my father asked to speak to her alone for a moment, Kosa looked to Perun, who refused. The behavior was not what he remembered, so he watched them."

"She doesn't listen to anyone. She would have spoken with Tannor. We both had fond memories of him." Jerina's suspicions were becoming stronger. Perun had control over her sister.

"One of Perun's servants told my dad that Kosa wasn't allowed to leave the house without his permission and then only with him. She must ask for everything. The servant also claimed to have seen Perun order her to use her magic when it seemed as if she didn't want to do it." Thane wasn't going to go into detail of how much her sister had been mistreated. Jerina didn't need to hear that.

Jerina wanted to cover her ears to block out what he was saying, but she needed to know. Somehow, Perun discovered one of the vila secrets.

Thane's scrutinizing stare bored into her. "You don't seem surprised about the level of control he has over her."

She ignored his comment. "Why are you telling me this? You wanted to turn me in to the Court last night."

He picked up a smooth pebble and skipped it across the water. "Perun had already gotten to the Court. Your sister made a complaint against you and asked for their protection. I couldn't seem to be on your side. I had to make you and everyone else believe that I agreed with them. It was the only way I could help you. They would have never allowed me to be your escort in town if they thought I was sympathetic to you."

He skipped another pebble. "It's all been an act. I needed you to dislike me and not want me to watch over you." Thane ran his hand through his hair again. "I needed you to not want to be around me. It was the only way to assure that I would be assigned to you."

Jerina sank onto the grass, suddenly feeling exhausted. Could she believe him? His arrogance and disdain were an act? She wiped her hands down her face. "I don't know what to believe. How do I know this isn't a game to get information from me?"

Thane clasped her hand and pulled her to her feet. "The grass is damp. Come back to the blanket."

Jerina followed along numbly. "How can I trust you?"

Thane held her gaze. "I'm going to help you rescue your sister."

Jerina was skeptical. "How?" She didn't trust him with what she feared.

"I'm going to help you get your sister's lock of hair back."

CHAPTER 7

*J*erina jumped to her feet, pulling her magically shortened sword from her pocket and willing it to its full and deadly length.

"How do you know about that?" she shouted.

Thane had been expecting her outburst, so he had a shield ready for when she advanced on him. "Easy."

"I'll make things really easy!" She imagined skewering him with her sword.

"We've been spying on Perun. He acquired a dark-magic-infused pocket watch from a dealer who doesn't worry about selling items legally. He bragged to the dealer that he needed it to hold a lock of hair that he didn't want to lose," Thane rushed out. "We started to do some research into vila legends. That's when we discovered your weakness."

"We don't have a weakness!" Jerina couldn't believe this was happening. She slid from the rock and backed away.

"Everyone has a weakness. I have a low tolerance for iron. All fae do. Every supernatural has something. Vampires can't tolerate the sun. Wolf shifters have trouble with silver. The vila just happen to have a weakness that can be exploited. You're immensely powerful, but can be controlled by a simple lock of hair." Thane shrugged.

"Perun is keeping Kosa's hair in his pocket watch, and we are going to get it back."

Jerina dropped her arm, pointing the sword to the ground. "How do I know you're not telling me this to get close enough to steal my hair?"

"I could have taken it from you many times, but I didn't. I won't." Thane was still in the same position, but he had dropped his shield. "I want to help you, but you need to start trusting me a little."

Jerina slumped. "What do you suggest we do?"

"We're going to break in to Perun's house and talk to your sister." Thane grinned at her when her mouth dropped open.

"Just like that? Go to his house, break in, and try to talk to my sister who is under his complete control?" Jerina growled her frustration. "You're insane!"

"Maybe a little." Thane stood and gathered up the blanket. "Come on, we need to start planning."

"You cannot be serious."

"Are you afraid of a little adventure?" Thane challenged.

Jerina narrowed her gaze. "Not at all. Let's go."

Four days later, Jerina was about to walk into the enemy's lair. She knew Thane had been working on a plan, but never expected it to be a trip into hostile territory dressed to kill.

"Now I know you're crazy," Jerina muttered as Thane tightened his hold on her hand, pulling her along the sidewalk leading up to Perun's Havenwood Heights mansion. "We're just going to walk up to the door and go inside?"

"How else do you suggest we enter? We could scale the ivy and crawl into the second-floor window, but I don't suggest you doing that in your evening gown." Thane was enjoying the red streaks across her cheeks and the fire in her eyes.

Jerina couldn't believe Thane's brilliant idea was to attend an upscale party at Perun's house. *What was he thinking?* "We're going to a ball at his house?"

"It was the perfect idea. Perun is hosting this year's spring Flower Ball fundraiser. Every supernatural in town will be in attendance. It would look odd if I didn't go, and I can't leave you unattended, so you had to come along." He gave her a toothy grin.

Jerina glanced down at the shimmering silver gown Thane had bought her from Callie's Trinkets and What Nots. The owner, Calla Lily Mircea, was so nice to Jerina when they arrived at her shop. Without any words, she immediately led Jerina over to a vintage silver dress that sparkled and insisted she try it on. It was exactly her size and the right style for the vila warrior.

Thane agreed that the dress was perfect. Jerina looked like a goddess ready to go to war. He laughed to himself because she *was* ready to do battle. She was carrying her sword with her in the small evening bag slung over her arm. He thought he saw her strap a knife or two under her gown.

Stopping, Thane turned to her and brought her in close to him so he could whisper quietly. "I know you're going to want to grab Kosa and take off or go after Perun. We can't do either. We are here to gather some information and hopefully give you and Kosa a few minutes to talk. If you lose control of your temper and cause a scene, we will be asked to leave, and you will be escorted from town. Can you keep it together?"

Jerina knew he was right, but it still irked her. "Yes. I'll be in control."

"Good." He leaned closer, his breath tickling her ear. "I'll be here to help you. Now let's put on a show." Thane's thumb was rubbing her hand in slow circles.

Jerina shivered, but not from fear. His breath and silky voice were giving her goose bumps. She had to stop herself from leaning into him. She shook herself. *What was she doing?* Vila needed to stay away from men.

Thane tucked her hand around his arm and led them forward. A few others were walking into the mansion. Flowers were everywhere they looked—lining the walkways, hanging from the trees in baskets, around the door in garlands, and on every windowsill. Wonderful fragrance filled the air along with a little magic. There were exotic flowers from all over the world, including many that were out of season. Jerina loved it.

A man at the door greeted them with an iris for Thane's lapel and a flower ring for Jerina's head. Each guest was given flowers to wear on their clothes, in their hair, or as jewelry. They continued through a blossom-covered archway and into the spacious foyer.

Perun, with Kosa on his arm, greeted the guests that lined up to enter the ball. Thane and Jerina stepped to the back of the line to wait their turn to say hello to their hosts.

Kosa's eyes grew large when she spotted her sister, but she quickly looked away. Thane noticed and squeezed Jerina's hand. She leaned closer. "I'm fine. I'm prepared for this."

"That's my girl." Thane winked, pulling her in closer to him. He could have continued their ruse of barely tolerating each other, but he decided it would be much more fun to act like lovers. It would throw everyone off.

The couple in front of them stepped away from Perun and Kosa, and then it was Thane and Jerina's turn. Perun took Jerina's hand and leaned over it, making a show of kissing her knuckles. It took everything she had not to pull her hand away and send him flying through the air.

"I'm surprised to see you here, my dear. I'm so happy you decided to accept my invitation to visit. I'm sure we can arrange for you to spend an extended amount of time here with your sister. You would like that, wouldn't you, Kosa darling?" Perun spoke loudly to all who were listening to the conversation.

Kosa blanched but simply nodded her head in agreement. A single tear ran down her face. Perun's eyes grew hard and dangerous. "Go powder your nose and come back," he whispered in her ear. "You may not speak to your sister."

Kosa glanced at Jerina and hurried off to do what she was told.

Thane tightened his hold on Jerina but was surprised to discover her in complete control of her powers and emotions. He grinned down at her.

"Your home is lovely. I can't wait to see what other flower displays you have," Jerina said loudly for the crowd and turned away.

Thane grinned at her. "Perun." He nodded his head. "Nice to see you."

"Watch her, Thane. Wouldn't want that one to get away from you."

Thane cocked his head to the side. "Don't worry about me. You have your own vila to worry about."

Thane didn't wait for a reply. He shuffled off with Jerina toward the ballroom.

Jerina stopped at a huge display of flowers that were designed to look like a volcano with lava erupting. It was amazing and looked so realistic. She liked looking at the flower art, but her mind was in the other room with her sister.

Jerina spotted Aspen and Tannor across the room. She hurried over to join them. Thane filled them in on what had been happening, and they agreed to help in any way they could. Aspen suggested that Jerina accompany her into the ladies' restroom.

Jerina frowned. "Why? Kosa can't speak to me."

"No, but you can speak to her, and she can answer back to me." Aspen grinned. "There is always a way around the problem. We elves are great at finding loopholes."

Aspen linked arms with Jerina to stop her from rushing off toward her sister. She was so excited at the prospect of speaking with her that Jerina practically ran through the hallways.

A few women were freshening up in the room that was filled with everything a lady might need to refresh at a party. Dozens of perfumes, hair sprays, makeup, and toiletries lined the counter under long mirrors. Jerina ignored it all and ventured into the back, where a secluded sitting area featured two love seats and a small table in between. The area was divided by privacy panels. It wasn't the best place, but it was better than nothing.

Aspen and Jerina approached Kosa, who was slumped over,

covering her face with both hands. It was obvious that she was weeping.

"Kos." Jerina reached out and gathered her sister in her arms. "It's going to be okay."

Kosa stiffened and tried to pull away, scanning the room frantically.

"Aspen is here with us. You can speak to her. He said you couldn't talk to me, but he never said that you couldn't speak to me through someone else."

Kosa wiped the tears from her eyes and tried to calm herself. She turned to Aspen. "I'm so sorry. Please tell her I'm so sorry."

Jerina stepped back so the three of them could gather closer together. "I know, Kosa. I'm going to figure out a way to get you out of here. Can you tell Aspen what happened? How he got you?"

Kosa focused on Aspen. "I went to tell him I wasn't going to see him anymore, but he tricked me. He wanted a hug goodbye. As soon as my arms went around him, I felt him tug on my hair. When I pulled away, he was dangling a long blond lock between his fingers. All I could do was stare at it. He was laughing manically, bragging how he now had all the power in the world. He was going to run the Green Coven and his hometown."

Wringing her hands, Kosa continued. "Perun's cousin, Ada, is the current leader of the Green Coven, and he hates that fact. He wants all of the coven's power to be his, but that won't happen unless he gets stronger. He's trying to use my magic and powers to do that."

"We'll get the hair back. He won't be able to control you anymore." Jerina didn't know how she was going to be able to do that, but she swore she wouldn't leave Havenwood Falls without her sister.

The sisters spoke through Aspen for a few more minutes, before Aspen warned that they were taking too long. She was afraid that Perun would send someone looking for Kosa.

Reluctantly, Jerina hugged her sister goodbye and promised to find a way to see her again.

Jerina was quiet when she returned to Thane's side, and he knew that he would have to do something to improve her mood if they were to keep up appearances. They needed to act like there was not a thing in the world wrong.

Saundra Beaumont and Sheriff Kasun were both in attendance, along with several other members of the Court. They all needed to see Jerina behaving herself and having a fun time.

Thane wrapped an arm around her shoulder and led her to the dance floor. Soft music played, and other couples were swaying to songs from Frank Sinatra, Bing Crosby, and Duke Ellington.

Jerina stopped on the edge of the floor and planted her feet, not moving another inch. "I don't know how to dance."

Thane rubbed her check. "It's just like a sword match, only without the blood and gore. Counter my moves, and you'll do just fine."

She considered him for a moment. "I think I can do that."

He leaned in. "You have to let me lead."

Jerina made a face, but moved closer and placed her left hand on his right shoulder like the other women were doing and her right hand in his left. Before she was ready, he began to move his feet. She stumbled at first, but he didn't seem to mind.

"Close your eyes. Feel what I'm doing and where I'm going. Let your body react naturally." Thane knew she would pick it up easily. She was so graceful when she moved and held a sword. Dancing was just more complex fighting steps.

A few minutes later, she opened her eyes and grinned up at him. "I like this."

"I knew you would. Wait until they play faster music. You'll love it even more." Thane would have liked to hear some of the faster big band tunes, but he was content to hold her and sway to the softer sounds.

"You don't seem to be having any more trouble," Perun remarked with Kosa in his arms, dancing alongside of them. "You must have discovered my secret for dealing with difficult women."

Thane's warning squeeze stopped anything Jerina might have said.

Thane smirked at Perun. "It's all about charm, my friend. The ladies love my charismatic wit and personality."

Perun laughed. "We'll have to talk after the festival tomorrow. I'm sure there is much to discuss."

Jerina wanted to zap him with some lightning, but she managed to turn away and pull Thane to a different area of the dance floor.

Thane leaned in to speak quietly in her ear. "You are doing amazingly well tonight. I'm proud of you. I know it took a lot of control not to go after him."

She didn't know why, but his praise thrilled her, and that scared the hell out of her.

CHAPTER 8

*C*olorful tents and booths filled the town square, displaying crafts, clothing, trinkets, jewelry, and floral designs. Areas were set up for flower-arranging lessons, seed swaps, children's crafts, gardening tips, and tons of food that were either made with plant ingredients or shaped to look like flowers. Another section held a stage where residents could vote on their favorite flowers and artwork.

Aspen was excited that her fuchsia-and-light-pink lily had been selected as a finalist. She had proudly displayed the plant in a hand-painted pot with a pink ribbon around it. Judging would continue throughout the day, and winners would be announced at the end of the festival.

Jerina scanned the crowd for her sister, but so far, Perun and Kosa had not made an appearance. "I thought Perun told you he would be here today?"

Thane glanced around. "He'll be here. He wants to know if I control you." Thane got a twinkle in his eyes. "We could always make him believe that I do. Are you up for a little acting?"

"No. Not happening." Jerina put her fists on her hips. She was not going to let him get away with bossing her around. He would have too much fun with it.

Tannor's arms were filled with items his wife had selected, while she only carried one bright yellow bouquet. "It might work, Jerina. I know what you're thinking. Thane won't take advantage of the situation, but Perun might speak more freely to Thane if he thought they were both reaping the same benefits from stolen hair."

Aspen piled another item on top of the others her husband held. "If he does step out of line, I'll help you get even with him."

"Mother!" Thane couldn't believe his own mother would side with Jerina.

Aspen chuckled, then stiffened slightly. "Perun is over there."

She shifted nervously and nibbled on one of the leaves of the blue Forget Me Nots she held in a pot in her arms.

Thane grinned when he saw his mom eating the flower. "Aren't you going to plant that?"

Aspen looked down. "Oh! Yes. It's going to be a part of the rock garden out back."

Tanner took the flowerpot from her. "You won't have anything to plant if you keep eating that." He turned to Thane and Jerina. "She was so nervous earlier, I had to take her flower entry away from her so she would still have something for the contest."

Thane leaned closer to Jerina and whispered in her ear. "Mom's an elf. They love to eat all kinds of plants. She starts snacking on leaves when she gets upset."

Jerina gave Aspen a half smile, but kept her eye on Perun.

Aspen shrugged. "I can't help it."

She nudged Tannor, and they left to find more flowers.

Jerina wanted to throw up. Kosa was clinging to Perun's arm, and he was parading her around like a trophy. He made a huge show of stopping to speak with everyone he passed in the crowd.

They were slowly making their way closer to Thane and Jerina. She knew she would have to act the part, so she gritted her teeth and wrapped her hand around his arm, staring up at him obediently.

"Don't blow a fuse, okay?" Thane joked. "Wouldn't want your head to explode."

"You fracture me." Jerina smiled sweetly. She had heard the

Petrans use that word when they thought something was funny and made them laugh.

Thane's eyebrows raised, surprised at the comment. She was beginning to fit into his world. "You're going to get even with me, aren't you?"

"You can count on it."

Thane rubbed his hands together. "Looking forward to it."

They watched Perun pass a few booths to get to the place where Thane and Jerina were standing. Thane pulled her a little closer. "Showtime."

Jerina plastered on a phony sweet smile and turned to face her sister, who looked terrified, and Perun, who was sporting a sinister smirk. Neither one of them had any flowers or crafts. It was clear to everyone that they had only attended the festival for social interaction. They were not supporting the local crafters and businesses.

"Good afternoon." Thane reached out his hand to shake Perun's.

"It's good to see you both enjoying the festival." Perun ran his knuckles across Kosa's cheek, watching Jerina for a reaction.

Thane was pleasantly surprised that Jerina did not attack Perun for touching her sister. He knew her restraint would not last too long if he didn't do something soon.

Perun rubbed Kosa's cheek again and licked his lips, all the while never taking his eyes from Jerina. "We should take a stroll through some of the judging tables."

Thane noticed the challenge in Perun's eyes, so he decided to test out the plan he and Jerina had created. Watching Perun from the corner of his eye, he addressed the vila on his arm. "Jerina, please go get the scoring sheets for the contests and bring them back quickly. Don't stop to speak with anyone. Run along now."

Kosa glanced between the two men in confusion.

Thane held his breath, hoping Jerina didn't zap him into the next county. With fire burning hotly in her eyes, she stomped off to do as he asked.

"NO!" sobbed Kosa, who slumped against Perun. He hadn't expected to support her weight, so she nearly sunk to the ground.

Jerina ground her teeth and trudged on. She hated the broken sound of her sister, but she knew they needed to play things right.

With her head down, she didn't make eye contact with anyone. She needed to do what he asked and return. Grabbing four score sheets and a few small pencils, she hurried back.

Kosa was sniffling beside Perun, who was scowling at her.

"Quiet down at once!" he hissed.

Thane wanted to punch the man, but he needed to keep his cool. Jerina was headed back to their group, and the next part of their plan needed to go perfectly. "I didn't know selecting the best flowers and crafts would be something you would want to do."

"I only like the best," Perun commented flippantly.

Thane grasped the opportunity.

"That's too bad, because it looks like I have the best this time." Thane reached his hand out to Jerina, who allowed him to pull her into his embrace. He held his arm around her back, locking her in place.

Jerina handed Thane the score cards. "Is there anything else you need?"

Thane scanned the crowd. "Yes. Do you see that man over there, across the square? I want you to blow his hat off his head but not have any wind blow across the booths."

Jerina raised her eyebrows in question, but did what he asked. She hoped he knew what he was doing. Raising her hand slightly, she focused on the man and directed a small amount of wind to whip by him, knocking his hat from his head. She hadn't done anything like that in a while, so she had a little fun with it. Once he bent to retrieve his hat, she blew it away again.

"That's enough," Thane chastened. He knew she enjoyed doing that, but he couldn't let Perun know that he wasn't in control of her.

Jerina cut off the wind and lowered her head to gaze at the ground. This meek act was driving her crazy.

Perun clapped his hands slowly and forcefully. "Congratulations. You have yourself a powerful weapon."

Thane didn't answer.

Perun stopped clapping to place his hand around the back of Kosa's neck. "We need to see a few more people before the festival is over."

Perun led Kosa away.

Jerina's eyes shot up with hatred flaring in their depths. Thane squeezed her side to offer the support he knew she must need from him. Seeing her sister in that situation must have been awful.

"You were amazing." Thane didn't know if his compliment would be met with hostility.

"It's a good thing you didn't ask me to do anything else. You would have been flying around with that man's hat." Jerina watched the crowd move, blocking her view of her sister.

"We needed to make him believe. My bet is he sends someone to my house to try to steal the hair he thinks I have. He wants control of both of you." Thane guided her toward a booth with displays of jewelry to distract her.

A snowflake with silver swirls around it caught her eye. She bent closer, drawn to the delicate charm.

"That reminds me of you." Thane picked it up carefully and held it to the light, watching it sparkle. He turned to the woman behind the table. "We'll take this."

Jerina's eyes shot to his. "You don't have to do that."

"I want you to have it. Someday, you'll be wearing it and I hope you'll think about me." Thane paid for the necklace, but didn't turn it over to Jerina. Instead, he stepped behind her to place it on her neck.

Jerina lifted her long blond hair so that he could secure it. She looked down and smiled. "Thank you." She sighed loudly. "Now what do we do?"

"We need to gather more information. Your sister should have it, if we can get to her."

"I've seen that look in your eyes. You are planning something."
Jerina studied him.

"How would you feel about being bait?"

CHAPTER 9

"*P*lease explain." Jerina wasn't afraid to put herself in danger. She just had to know all the details.

"The Green Coven meets once a month in a different coven member's house. After the meeting, several of them will go to one of the local pubs for a few drinks. Perun usually goes to flirt with the female tourists or human residents. It might be the perfect time for you to distract him while I sneak in to speak with Kosa." Thane had tried to think of as many things that could go wrong as possible.

Jerina's eyes grew into saucers. "You think that's safe?"

Thane didn't love the idea of splitting up from Jerina, but he needed to get inside Perun's mansion without him being there. "I don't want you to go alone, but it's the only way we can keep Perun distracted and still get to speak with your sister."

Jerina frowned. "I cannot go anywhere in town without someone coming with me."

Thane guided her toward another booth as they made their way to the food vendors. "I thought of that. Calla Lilly was just telling me that she needed a night out."

"She would do that for me?" Jerina couldn't believe that someone she barely knew would help her so much. Then she looked at Thane and realized that he was helping her more than she had any right to expect. They were playing a dangerous game, and he had no thought for himself. He only wanted to help her.

Thane noticed the change in her expression. "Is everything okay?"

She stared up at him. "Yes." She tried to pull her eyes away from him, but he held her captive.

Thane cupped her chin. "We'll get your sister back."

She nodded. "I know. I trust you."

Fire ignited in Thane's eyes, and he tightened his hold on her, his eyes glued to hers. He slowly bent his head toward her, but stopped inches away, waiting to see her reaction.

She tilted her head toward his, aligning their lips, daring to take what he was offering. Just as his mouth was about to settle on hers, they were jostled apart by a group of teens pushing past. Jerina hastily stepped back and shook herself out of the spell he had cast on her.

A blush streaked her cheeks, but she didn't look away from him.

"Come on. I want to show you something." He linked his fingers through hers and pulled her along as he weaved through the crowd.

Slipping into an alley between two of the large buildings, he crossed behind Whisper Falls Inn and continued jogging a few blocks until they reached Danzan Park. He had a sudden need to not share her with anyone else.

The park was empty, with most of the town residents at the flower festival. Thane led her past a few trees and backed her against a large trunk that blocked everyone from view.

A warning was flashing in Jerina's head, but she was too tempted by Thane to heed it. She wanted to explore things with him a little bit. Surely the curse would allow her a few minutes of passion.

Thane's predatory gaze should have made her nervous, but it thrilled her instead. She wasn't sure what he had planned, but she was ready for whatever happened.

He had been holding back, waiting for her to show some faith in him. To trust him. He could still hear her saying those words.

Sliding both hands into her hair, he held her gently, giving her time to push him away. She didn't. She fisted his jacket and pulled him closer to her.

Thane dipped his head down, nudging her nose with his as his lips inched closer to hers.

Jerina's heart thundered in her ears as she waited for his mouth to settle over hers. She'd had a few kisses in her life, but they were simply to sate her curiosity about men. She had never found any particularly interesting enough to dally with.

Thane couldn't wait any longer. He claimed her lips in a searing kiss that was sure to burn him into her memory forever. His teeth grazed her lip, nipping it playfully, before his tongue swept inside her mouth to meet hers.

As soon as his mouth laid claim to hers, Jerina wrapped her arms around his neck and held on as wave after wave of emotion burst forth. If a kiss was this amazing, what would more be like?

Thane shifted his hold, pulling her closer and deepening the kiss. He knew it would be good between them, but he never dreamed it would be this intense.

Jerina broke the kiss, breathing deeply, chest heaving as she fought for control.

Thane leaned his forehead against hers and closed his eyes. "I won't apologize for that."

Jerina smiled. "I won't ask you to."

He caught her eye. "It's going to happen again."

Jerina placed her hand on his cheek. "We can't let this go too far."

Thane straightened and took a couple of steps back. "Why not?"

Covering her face with her hands, she struggled for control of her raging emotions. The wind whipping through the trees was growing in intensity.

Thane pulled her hands away from her face.

"Why not?" he repeated.

Jerina sucked air into her lungs. "Because we are cursed."

Thane shrugged. "I know that."

Shaking her head, she backed up a couple of feet. "No. Not about our hair. We have another curse."

Thane dropped his shoulders. "I'm not talking about your hair."

Jerina wanted to stomp her feet. He needed to listen to her. "Thane, you don't understand! You could die! I don't want anything to happen to you! Vila are cursed to never find true love. If we do, our true love will die a terrible death."

Thane closed the distance between them and framed her face with his hands. "I already know that is the legend. The vila believe it, but I don't."

Jerina grabbed his wrists to pull his hands from her face, but she just held him in place. "You know our legends are true. You've seen the power Perun has over Kosa by just having a lock of her hair. This is true too."

Thane's thumbs caressed her cheeks. "Haven't you ever heard that true love conquers all or true love's kiss breaks the spell? There is nothing stronger than true love. I believe it. True love brought my father back to my mom after he was wounded in World War I."

Jerina dropped her hands to his jacket. "True love didn't bring him home. I did."

He slid his hands farther into her hair. "How do you know that true love didn't send you to help him?"

"We can't let this go any further. I like you too much. I don't want anything to happen to you." Jerina wondered if it was already too late. She was growing attached to the charming, arrogant male.

"I'm not going anywhere, and I won't let you push me away." Thane wrapped his arms around her and hugged her tightly.

"I can't push you away right now. You're my assigned escort while I'm in Havenwood Falls." Jerina clung to him, absorbing some of his strength.

Since she was still in his arms, he kissed her again to remind her just how good it was between them.

After what seemed like hours, Thane walked her back to the inn and stopped at the bottom of the staircase. "Good night, Jerina. Sweet dreams." Thane winked at her. "Of me."

~

It had been three days since Thane had kissed her in the park and two days since she had seen her sister in town on Perun's arm.

Jerina had met Calla Lily for a drink at the Fallview Tavern. It was the hangout of the Green Coven since Ada Daryn, the coven's leader, controlled the sirens who ran the place. They entered the building with high ceilings, wooden beam supports, and hardwood floors. Everything seemed to be covered in earth tones with a large iron chandelier hung over the sitting area in front of the stone fireplace. Iron was everywhere, so she understood why Thane didn't step inside.

While they were waiting for Perun to arrive, they discovered that the Green Coven meeting had been postponed. It had been a nice night with a new friend, but it hadn't accomplished what she wanted.

Thane stayed outside Perun's mansion for hours until it was clear. He wasn't leaving Kosa alone. He wondered if Perun had discovered their plans. He wasn't sure how that would be possible, but it was too coincidental for his liking.

The next day, they had heard the Green Coven was going to meet. They prepared once again to distract Perun so Thane could speak privately with Kosa.

Jerina was supposed to only let Perun see her, but she would do whatever was necessary to give Thane time to do what he needed to do. Once again, she was wearing a vintage dress from Calla Lily's shop. This one was a little more daring than she normally wore, but Thane assured her that she looked amazing in it. The bright red A-line dress barely reached her knees, and its open collar dipped lower than any of her other clothes.

She kept glancing down to make sure the top of her dress was where it was supposed to be. Madame Luiza had told her it was not indecent and that it was designed to make a man wonder what the clothes were hiding. Jerina could picture the leer spreading across Perun's face when he saw her.

This time, Jerina was going to the Fallview Tavern with Irina and Mihail Petran. Normally, she would hate tagging along with a couple, but it would work to her benefit if Perun noticed her.

Thane stopped by before they left to wish her luck and to warn her not to engage Perun without him there. She didn't plan to take on Perun herself, so she agreed.

The tavern was crowded, but the three of them found a few soft chairs around a small table next to the bar where they could survey the entire place. They had been there for half an hour when Perun strode in with two other men who Jerina could tell were also mages. They oozed much more power than Perun.

Jerina understood where his obsession began. Perun wanted to be like his coven mates, but his level of power didn't come close. He wanted to use her sister to compete with the others. Disgust filled her.

Mihail drew Irina from her chair and brought her to the dance floor, leaving Jerina by herself. They had planned to do this as soon as they knew Perun was in the bar. It had been Irina's idea, and Jerina readily agreed. They also suggested that no one mention the change of plans to Thane. He might not like the risk Jerina was taking.

Jerina sipped on a gin and tonic, watching the single patrons flirt and the older gentlemen sway on their stools from too many alcoholic beverages. She loved to people-watch, and the tavern was a great place to do that.

She was going to pretend not to notice Perun, but she decided to be bold and stare him down. Perun was attracted to the strong and powerful. He would seek her out.

"Where is your keeper?" Perun demanded.

"He left someone else to watch over me, as you can see." Mihail and Irina stopped dancing to stare over. They were waiting for Jerina to let them know if she needed their help. "Where is my sister?"

"Locked in her room," he sneered. "Want to join her there?"

Jerina laughed. "And be under your control?"

"I know you're here to see me." Perun's eyes were glued to the V neckline of her dress.

It took every ounce of willpower to not smack the leer from his face. "Of course I am. I am drawn to you." Jerina couldn't stop her eyes from rolling.

Perun's leer intensified. "I should have held out for the fiery one. Maybe Thane will make a switch." He stepped closer to her.

Jerina saw her shot and decided to go for it. She leaned a little closer to him. "You think you could handle me?"

Perun licked his lips. "I look forward to proving it to you."

Jerina placed her hand on his chest. "Thane would never give you the chance." She slipped her hand lower.

Perun adjusted his stance, moving the bulge in his pants. "We might share you both. He seems to like a variety of women."

Jerina swallowed her disgust. She could do this. "He doesn't share, but I do."

She slid her hand lower still. She rested it just above Perun's vest pocket. She could feel the evil power radiating from the watch. Her hand was so close.

She fluttered her eyelashes at him like she had seen women do in the movie that Thane had taken her to a few days before. Jerina had no idea how to flirt, but Perun seemed to like what she was doing.

"I've never had sisters before. Do you and Kosa share everything?" He was leaning into her and breathing harder.

Jerina wanted to gag, but she kept a slight smile on her face. She licked her lips to keep his eyes on her face and slid her fingers into his pocket.

Perun grabbed her hand, crushing her fingers until they felt like they would break into a million pieces. "Do you think I am that stupid? Did you think you could fool me with that poor attempt at flirting?"

He pushed her away from him, toppling her chair and leaving her sprawled out on the floor. Perun stormed from the tavern in a rage.

Jerina jumped up and ran from the bar to follow him. She knew he would go directly to her sister.

CHAPTER 10

$\mathcal{T}$hane crept up to the historic mansion in the heart of the old-money district. He was sure hoping that none of the founding families on the street saw what he was about to do. He would be brought in front of the Court, and then he would have to answer a whole bunch of questions he wasn't ready for.

He had been teasing Jerina at the ball about climbing up the ivy and crawling into a window, but that was exactly what he was going to do. The trestle that supported the vines reached up to the second floor of the majestic home. He knew Kosa was staying on the higher floor in a servant's room. Perun didn't want her to get any ideas that she was anything but a servant to him.

He was purposely dressed in all black so he would blend with the night and wore sturdy climbing boots. Thane could hear someone listening to the radio loudly, which served his purposes. No one would hear him if he fell off the ivy.

A night watchman strolled down the street whistling, assuring that any criminal would hear him approaching and hide away safely. Thane chuckled to himself. The guy had no plans to look for anyone up to no good, and if he did unwittingly run into a crime in progress, he would probably turn and run the other way.

Shaking his head, he began to climb the greenery. Between the trellis and the twisted vine, climbing was way easier than he thought it would be. He reached the second-floor window that he was told would be open by the servant that had been feeding him information about Perun. The window raised with ease, and Thane was able to slip inside the room. He dropped down to the floor and paused to listen to the sounds of the house.

All was quiet, so he continued on to the hallway. According to the servant that his father paid, Kosa would be locked in a room one floor up and just down the hall to the left. He needed to be careful to avoid any servants who were ordered to stand guard.

He hoped there weren't any outside her door. He was prepared to deal with it if that turned out to be the case, but he would rather not have to.

Thane made it to the servants' steps at the back of the house without seeing anyone. He had heard a few voices inside rooms, but no one had ventured out into the hallway. He knew at least two of the servants had been rather busy with each other from the sound of it.

As soon as he reached the top floor, he leaned out quickly to see if anyone was there. Cursing to himself, he realized someone was just outside Kosa's door. He would have to throw a sleeping spell on the guard and hope it lasted long enough for him to get to Kosa, speak with her, and leave.

Thane leaned out again and saw the large man leaning against the wall, listening to the radio and not paying much attention to anything else. Thane was thankful he wouldn't have to confront the man who was at least a half a foot taller than Thane's six-foot-two frame. The man had about fifty pounds on him too.

Thane whispered some words that would put the man to sleep and waited for a thump. It never came. Thane leaned out again, and the man was still in the same position as he was before, wide awake.

Frowning, he said the spell again, but with more power behind it. He didn't hear the man slump to the floor.

"What the hell?" Thane mumbled to himself. He was going to have to find another way inside her room.

Returning to the second floor, he counted the rooms and stopped at the one just below Kosa. He listened at the door, but didn't hear anything. He slowly twisted the knob and entered the room. It was a guest bedroom that didn't look like it had been used in years. The furnishing and decor were from decades past.

Thane approached the window and slid it open to look out. The trellis didn't reach that high, but the ivy did. He would have to take a chance at climbing it to her window. He just hoped Kosa was awake and not completely freaked out to have someone at her window at night.

The climb was relatively uneventful. He managed to slip only twice, but the ivy was so thick he was able to find another foothold quickly. Being half elf, he had an affinity with plants, so he encouraged it to grow and strengthen to help his climb. The ivy was happy to oblige.

He reached her window and was thankful that she was sitting up in bed with her nightstand lamp on. Thane tapped lightly, trying not to draw too much attention. Impatiently waiting, he tapped again. He saw Kosa stiffen and hop out of bed to investigate. She cautiously approached the window and frowned at him, ready to knock him off the ivy.

"What are you doing here?" she hissed.

Thane held up his hands in surrender. "I'm here to help. Your sister sent me."

Kosa moved closer to the window. "How do I know that's true?"

"She told me to tell you that she hasn't forgotten you pushing her out of the tree, and when you both get back home, you should beware." Thane repeated what Jerina had told him. "She also said that I might be an arrogant crumb, but you should listen to me. I'm here to help." He shrugged. "She's not entirely correct about that part. I'm not a crumb."

Kosa arched a brow in an expression that was so much like her sister. "Are you in control of her?"

Thane chuckled. "I don't think anyone would ever be in control of Jerina."

She was satisfied enough with his answers. Kosa unlocked the window and slid it open so he could enter. Kosa held a finger in front of her lips. "We need to be quiet. Someone is right outside the door."

Thane nodded. "I saw him. I tried to spell him to sleep, but my magic wasn't working."

Kosa sat him down on the floor on the window side of her bed so they were somewhat hidden. "Perun bragged that he was immune to magic and had some sort of innate protection against spells. That was why he was put there. My magic won't work against him."

"How do you know that?" Thane asked.

Kosa shrugged. "We have a drink together every night. He likes to share."

Thane looked thoughtful. "Interesting. You've got moxie. I'll give you that." He sat on the floor, facing the door. He was ready to defend them if necessary, but had a feeling she could take care of herself. "I'm Thane. We haven't been properly introduced. I'm helping your sister."

Kosa growled at him. "You'd better be helping her, because even the gods won't be able to help you if you're lying to me."

Thane loved how fiercely loyal they were to each other. "I would never hurt her. I'd do anything to make sure she was happy and safe. Even scale a building to gather information to save her sister."

Kosa studied him, suddenly understanding. "You're falling for her, aren't you?"

Thane didn't answer.

"Do you know about the curse?" Kosa asked gently, terrified for her sister. They could never have true love.

"Yes, but I don't believe it." Thane crossed his arms over his chest.

"You should. We've seen it happen before." Kosa tried to shift to a more comfortable position, but the floor was hard.

"I'm not here to discuss a curse. I'm here to talk to you about Perun. Do you know where he keeps his pocket watch?" Thane leaned back against the wall.

"When it's not in his pocket, it's in a box on his dresser. I've seen it before a few times." Kosa didn't think there was any way to get the watch.

Thane grinned. This was the information he needed. "Describe it to me. I need every detail you can remember."

Kosa had her first smile in a long time. "I can show you."

One of her gifts was sharing memories. She could connect with someone and allow them to witness something she had seen or done. It was never something she valued until now.

Kosa closed her eyes and pictured what she wanted Thane to see. Grasping his wrist, she drew him into her vision.

Just as her memory ended, they heard Perun's raised voice down the hallway. Thane quickly slid into her closet. There was not enough time for him to open the window and climb outside.

He heard Perun enter Kosa's room and pull her forcefully into the hallway. He waited a few minutes to make sure he wouldn't be seen or heard and left through the window. He was going to follow after them.

CHAPTER 11

*T*he darkened street was deserted, with most of its residents already asleep. Jerina hadn't expected to be caught following Perun home and never imagined that he would drag Kosa outside to punish her in front of Jerina. He was taking his fury out on Kosa when it should have been directed at Jerina.

Jerina was the one who had attempted to flirt with him to steal the pocket watch, and she was the one who had been caught in the act.

"I know you're watching, Jerina! Step into the moonlight so I can see you. I wouldn't want you to miss this," Perun taunted, pulling Kosa along after him.

Kosa stumbled twice but managed to keep up with his punishing pace.

"Come see what happens to Kosa when you defy me!" Perun backhanded Kosa across the face, sending her sprawling into a row of hedges.

"No! Leave her alone!" Jerina screamed, losing all control over her emotions. She knew she should walk away and find Thane, but she wouldn't leave her sister to this despicable mage.

Leaves began to rustle, thunder roared in the distance, Jerina's hair blew back, and she was gathering lightning. She wished she could simply blast him, but his mage magic and her sister's powers would block any attempt she made. She would have to catch him without Kosa around and without him realizing what was happening.

"I knew you were here." He turned to Kosa. "Come here. I'm not finished with you."

Jerina watched Kosa slump over and gather something in her nightgown. Kosa stomped up to Perun and faced him unafraid.

Kosa's eyes met Jerina's seconds before Kosa grabbed the branch she had hidden in her nightgown and attempted to whack Perun in the head. He might have control over her, but she would fight him until the end. She would not accept her fate.

Perun's temper flared out of control when he blocked the strike. He swung his fist back and let it fly into Kosa's cheek, nearly knocking her out.

Kosa grabbed her throbbing cheek and sobbed her frustration and pain. Perun roughly pulled her up and led her from the street and away from Jerina, laughing the entire way.

Jerina was left on the street alone.

Wind whipped through the trees, lightning blazed across the sky, and a torrent of rain and hail crashed down on the entire region. Jerina's scream of outrage echoed through the valley as she watched Perun lead her sister away.

A hurricane was forming over their valley, and there was nothing Jerina could do to stop it.

Strong arms circled her from behind, and at first, she struggled until she heard his soft murmurs in her ear. "It's going to be okay. Jerina, you must stop this. They'll know it's you. I figured out a way to rescue her. Kosa won't be with him much longer, but I need your help!"

Jerina's whole body shook from uncontrollable rage.

"Please, babe, you need to listen. I know how to save her." Thane pleaded, but his words were not getting through to her. There was only one thing he could think of that might work.

Thane twisted her around and claimed her mouth in a searing, branding kiss that was designed to curl her toes. He slanted his mouth over hers, taking ownership and demanding that she participate.

The rain soaked through their clothes, but neither of them paid any attention to it. She was unresponsive at first, but he claimed victory when her arms wound around his neck and the wind died down. As he continued to kiss her and his tongue explored her mouth, the external storm dissipated.

Thane's hands ran up and down her back, getting to know her every curve. When he pulled her closer and considered exploring her body more, he pulled away panting.

Jerina's pupils were dilated and her breath ragged, but she no longer affected the weather. "He hit her."

Thane hugged her harder. "I know. I saw." He rubbed her back in soothing circles. "We're going to rescue her and make sure he pays."

"How?" The rain turned to a drizzle that eventually stopped. Jerina was regaining control.

Thane winked at her. "I have a plan."

His plan was simple. Executing it would prove to be a little bit harder. Everything had to be perfect, or it wouldn't work. He knew magic would play a big part and so would an elaborate illusion, but they also needed a fairly big distraction and lots of luck.

Thane was thankful that Kosa was able to share her memories of the box that Perun kept on his dresser and of the pocket watch itself. Those recollections were key to his plan.

A stop at Simple Treasures Pawn Shop—owned by Lawrence Mills, a dragon shifter and Court member—gave him a little bit more to think about, but he was sure things would work out. He purchased a couple of items he would need to pull off his plan.

An hour later, Thane picked Jerina up at the inn and led her across the town square.

"Where are we going?" Jerina fidgeted nervously, not liking the direction they were headed.

"We have an important meeting."

Jerina stopped dead. "I'm not going in there!"

Thane pulled on her hand to get her moving. "You don't have a choice. They're waiting for us."

Jerina groaned. "This won't go well."

Sheriff Kasun met them at the back door of City Hall once again. Instead of scowling, he simply nodded. Jerina had no idea what to make of that.

"Follow me." Without waiting for them to respond, he turned and headed down the steps to go into the basement of the building.

He stopped before a set of double doors that led to the main meeting room. Jerina didn't want to go in there.

Thane rubbed her hand with his thumb. "You trust me, right?"

Jerina took a deep breath. "Yes."

"Good. Let's go."

The members of the Court were already assembled in their seats. They were speaking quietly amongst themselves, but stopped all conversations when Thane and Jerina entered.

Thane inclined his head. "Thank you for agreeing to meet with us. As I was explaining before and with evidence from a reliable eye witness, Perun has stolen a lock of Kosa's hair and has taken control of her."

Jerina shifted from foot to foot. She didn't think they would listen to what they had to say and would simply kick her out before she could get Kosa away from the evil mage.

Thane continued. "I provided information on vila from our town library, and we have a vila warrior here to answer any of your questions."

Saundra leaned forward. "Why didn't you explain all of this when you arrived?"

"I didn't know he had control of her then. I had hoped she was only angry with me for wanting her to discontinue seeing an admirer." Jerina met Saundra's stare with ease. She was not afraid of the truth.

"And after you discovered the truth?" Saundra continued.

"I didn't think you would believe me. You made it very clear that you thought I would be a trouble maker so I didn't hold much faith that your opinion of me would change," Jerina countered. She heard a few grumbles, but no one said anything about her statement.

Jerina continued. "The vila keep to ourselves, so not much is widely known about us. We also don't like to announce a weakness, so I didn't think Perun would know about it. He must have done a lot of research."

"How do you know he has her hair?" Saundra and the Court wanted to hear it from her even though they had already received information from Thane.

Thane nodded to her to keep going with her story.

"He orders her around and demands she do things that she ordinarily wouldn't do. He told her she couldn't speak to me, but we figured out a way to do it through Aspen."

Another Court member, Roman, made a disbelieving sound. "That's not proof."

Jerina glared at him. "He made her go sit down by herself and not talk to anyone. He demanded she use her powers when it was obvious she didn't want to, and he also beat on her in front of me and she had to stand there and take it!"

Saundra shifted uncomfortably. "He abused her?"

Jerina was shaking with rage, but she was keeping it together enough to not affect the weather. "He backhanded her and then punched her in the face. As he pulled her away with him, he yelled at her to stop crying."

Thane rubbed the small of her back. "I have spoken with Kosa, and she confirmed that Perun has her hair."

Saundra sighed. "Thane, please tell us what you have planned."

Jerina interrupted. "You'll help us?"

Roman leaned forward to glare at her. "No. We will not."

Saundra frowned. "What Roman means is that we won't

interfere with your rescue attempt, but we also cannot offer you any assistance."

Jerina turned to walk out of the meeting room, but Thane grasped her arm to stop her. "Just wait a few minutes," he whispered.

"Why?" she demanded in a normal voice.

"Please. You trust me."

"I knew I'd regret telling you that." Jerina kicked him in his calf and returned to standing next to him.

Saundra cleared her throat, not happy with the disruption.

Thane stood straighter. "We need a little assistance with some spells that will mimic dark magic and that will also contain it."

Saundra looked stern. "That could be arranged."

Thane held up a wrapped package. "It would be great if you could do that now."

Saundra narrowed her gaze but waved them closer.

The sun had barely risen when Jerina ventured outside of the inn and into the back gardens. She couldn't sleep and had too much nervous energy, so she needed to find something to do. It had been so long since she practiced with her sword, so she pulled it out and began to swing it in sweeping arcs.

Jerina shifted back and forth with her moves in a combination of arm and foot work. Having her sword in her hand gave her comfort.

"You're up early."

Jerina hadn't seen Thane enter the garden. He smirked as he pulled his two short swords from a sheath on his back.

She grinned up at him, readying her sword.

"Something told me you would want some fun this morning." Thane twisted his swords in an elaborate pattern.

Jerina admired his graceful movements and was mesmerized by the way his muscles rippled and pulled across his arms and chest. Caught staring at his body, she didn't see the sword coming toward her until it was right in front of her face. She swung her sword up to catch it, and the sparring was on.

Parrying across the grass and pathways, and through the flower beds, they clashed swords and strikes. Jerina had seen him fight her younger warriors, but he had been holding back. Fighting him was thrilling and challenging. She hadn't had a match like this in years.

After a while, they both decided to end things before their competitive streaks took over and one of them got hurt. As it was, Thane had a cut across his thigh, and Jerina's shirt sleeve had a couple of torn spots with beads of blood seeping through.

Thane replaced his swords and sat down on the dirt path, trying to catch his breath. Jerina had been the best opponent he had ever had. He couldn't wait to practice with her again.

"How did you know I was out here?" Jerina asked, wiping sweat from her forehead with her sleeve.

"I know you." Thane grinned at her.

"You think you know me so well?" Jerina teased.

He nodded, rising to reach her side. He only wanted to brush back some of the strands of hair that were sticking to her check, but he ended up caressing her neck down to her shoulder.

Her shivering response was all the encouragement he needed. Bending his head, he nipped at her lip before pressing his mouth gently against hers. The kiss was feather soft and sweet, intended to only savor the moment, but once he started, he craved more.

Jerina tugged on his shirt to get him closer. She knew she shouldn't allow him to kiss her, but it was too intoxicating and wicked to stop.

Thane broke his mouth away from hers but placed a quick peck on her forehead. "We need to get cleaned up. We have a big day. I'll be back in a couple of hours."

Jerina nodded and watched him walk off. She had a ton of things to do before they executed their plan that night.

CHAPTER 12

Thane had snuck in to see Kosa again to explain what they had planned. She was more than willing to help and even offered a suggestion as to how they should distract Perun. She had been gathering as much information about him as she could in hopes that she would one day be free of him. She knew Jerina wouldn't give up on her, but she never expected Thane to be just as dedicated to saving her.

Every night after she was locked inside her room, she would peek under the bed to see if Thane had left anything for her. The first night, she found a key that seemed to be infused with magic. She discovered that it unlocked every door she tried. That would be a handy thing to have.

She found a spell to counteract the dark magic in the pocket watch enough for her to take it. They were not sure if it would be powerful enough to allow them to destroy it.

The next night, she found a small corked glass bottle with instructions on how to use it to make the guard outside her door fall asleep. It was a strong sleeping draught that doctors used on humans. If he was immune to magic, maybe pharmaceuticals would work. There was enough for two times. Once to test it out and once to use on him when they planned their rescue, if it worked the first time. She would slip it into his drink and hope for the best.

Kosa could hardly wait for her next instruction.

Thane and Jerina had made sure that Perun and Kosa were occupied at one of the restaurants in town before they broke into his house. They needed to leave a package for Kosa.

It had been anticlimactic and disappointing to Jerina. They had walked up to the back door, recited an open spell, entered the house, and ran up the back stairs without seeing anyone. She didn't want any trouble or danger, but she had expected something a little more interesting.

They left a carved wooden box trimmed in gold swirls with gold hinges and lock. It was an exact replica of Perun's box. Even if it had slight differences, the magical illusion covering it would assure that he saw only his box.

Inside the box was a gold pocket watch that was spelled to look and feel just like Perun's. Saundra had helped to make the watch carry a dark magic signature so that it would give off the same energy as his.

It was vital that when Kosa switched out the boxes, he believed that he still had his originals.

Thane picked up the white silk wrap and stepped behind Jerina. She twisted around to view him, surprised at the gentlemanly gesture. She had never experienced a man helping her do anything. She allowed him to place the wrap around her shoulders and was thankful she could suppress a shudder when his fingers brushed her neck as he pulled her hair from beneath the wrap.

Thane shrugged. "Since we are all spiffy, I figured I'd better pull out my good manners."

Jerina glanced at him, at a loss.

Thane grinned at her discomfort. "It's just a short walk to Glitz. We have reservations for the ten o'clock show. We have a little bit of time to walk around the town square."

"What is Glitz?" Jerina linked her arm through his as they left the inn.

"It's a restaurant with a big band and two couples that sing and dance. Some say that one of the girls is a better dancer than Ginger Rogers." Thane knew his parents enjoyed going there on a night out on the town. He would have liked to take Jerina out on a real date, but that wouldn't happen until Kosa was safe.

"Who is Ginger Rogers?" Jerina crinkled her forehead.

Thane smiled. "She's an actress and one of the best dancers today. My mom will have a photo of her in one of her magazines."

Thane and Jerina walked through the town square as if nothing was wrong in the world. They meandered through the crowds, window-shopped, and chatted with people as they walked by. No one would ever suspect that in an hour, they were going to break into Perun's house, steal the watch, and rescue Kosa.

Jerina paused to glance inside Charms Soda Shoppe, her favorite place to get ice cream. She wished they weren't on a mission and had time to enjoy themselves with dessert.

They had decided to sit in the gazebo for a few minutes to calm Jerina's emotions enough for them to continue on with their plans.

Glitz was a couple of blocks off the square, sitting majestically up on a hill. Valets waited in front of the circular drive to hop into the convertibles and luxury vehicles of the town's exclusively wealthy.

Jerina watched as glamorous women in sparkling gowns and high heels clung to the arms of dashing men in suits and fedora hats.

"Do they always dress like this?" Jerina asked, feeling a little out of place.

Thane turned her toward him as they watched a maroon Pontiac Streamliner pull up to the valet station followed closely behind by a shiny red DeSoto sedan.

"Most of the people that come here do." He brushed hair from her cheek. "Don't worry. You look beautiful."

She simply smiled, not knowing what to say to the compliment. Bright lights lit the entire area, making it almost like daylight as people filtered into the restaurant. Jerina glanced at the two-story glass front of the building that sparkled and gleamed in the brightness.

Jerina caught the eyes of two young human men who were trailing behind an older couple.

"Check out the dish over there," she heard one of them say to his friend.

"She's a looker. Too bad she's with that tall fella." The other guy was not hiding his blatant stare.

Thane placed his hand at the small of her back and guided her inside and away from the men. He focused on Jerina and not the two outside.

"Thane?" Jerina called for the third time.

He smiled sheepishly. "Sorry. It's taking all my self-control not to go out there and brain those two."

"Brain?" His words sometimes confused her.

"It means hit on the noggin." Thane pointed to his head.

"There's no need for that." Jerina turned toward the two women waiting to greet them. One of them approached and helped Jerina remove her wrap, and the other took Thane's hat and overcoat. The lobby was filled with lounge chairs in cozy clusters, allowing for privacy while patrons waited to be seated.

Thane had phoned ahead and arranged for them to have a table at the side of the room that offered a little privacy. They left the lobby, venturing down a few steps into the vast main ballroom. A large low stage covered the back wall, with a raised platform off to the right that held the big band. White linen tables with crystal wine glasses rimmed the dance floor in the center of the room.

Jerina was captivated by everything she saw. They were led to a table at the edge of the room that was set for two. Thane pulled out her chair and waited as she took her seat.

"Thank you," she said nervously. They would be sneaking out of the show soon, but she was determined to enjoy things while they lasted.

"I'm sorry we can't stay and see the entire show. I will bring you back here after we save Kosa." Thane was busy watching Jerina as she took everything in with the innocence and wonder of someone experiencing everything for the first time.

She bestowed him with a dazzling smile. "I would love that."

The lights turned low, and music filled the room. Thane knew they could stay for a few minutes of the show before sneaking off.

Jerina sat up in her seat with her eyes glued to the stage. A couple of women danced into the center of the stage from the sides, swirling their long gowns to the beat. Their dance partners swept them into their arms and continued to twirl them around so many times, Jerina would have become dizzy.

After a couple of songs, Thane reached over and laced his fingers with hers. "We have to go."

Jerina nodded and slowly stood, sliding along the wall to the rear exit. Thane followed behind quietly. Thankfully no one was paying attention to the dimly lit outer area. It would be easy to leave while the performance was underway.

Thane unlocked the door with magic, and they hurried into the alleyway.

Step one of their plan had been completed.

The walk to Perun's hadn't taken much time at all, so they arrived before Thane had anticipated getting there. That gave them extra time to make sure everything was in place.

Kosa left the curtains to her room open and the light on so they could see inside. She walked past the window twice but didn't look outside. They knew once she knocked the guard out cold, she would signal that she was ready.

"I hate waiting," Jerina mumbled. "It makes me antsy."

Thane leaned over and kissed her forehead. "I could come up with something to keep your mind off of things."

She glanced sideways at him. "No, thank you."

"Your loss." Thane purposely ran his hand down the length of her arm as he reached around her to look into their bag. They had brought a few weapons with them in case things turned out badly. They hoped it wouldn't happen, but they needed to be prepared.

Kosa stood at the window, looking out for several moments and then turned out the light. That was the signal.

"How do we know if Perun is asleep?" Jerina asked.

"He won't be. It's still early enough that he will be in bed, but not asleep. That's where my part comes in." Thane kissed her cheek and jogged off toward the front door.

It was an indecent time to call on someone, but Thane was counting on that. He needed Perun to be already dressed for bed and annoyed at having to answer the door.

Thane knocked loudly on the front door for several minutes. A haggard looking man answered the door with a sharp, "May I help you, sir?"

Thane brushed by him and into the foyer. "I must see Perun at once. It's urgent."

The servant seemed torn between rushing off after his employer and ejecting Thane from the house.

"Hurry!" Thane insisted. He even made a show of pacing back and forth.

Perun appeared at the top of the staircase, wrapping a silk robe over his cotton pajamas. "What is it? This had better be important, Thane!"

Thane tried extremely hard not to grin. His plan was working out perfectly. "I needed to speak with you at once."

"What is it?" Perun's exasperation was clear.

"I found a loophole with controlling vila with their hair. It's a way out for them. I needed to warn you immediately."

Perun narrowed his gaze at Thane and exhaled a deep breath. "Why are you sharing this with me?"

"Jerina escaped. I'm going to get her back. I figured she would probably go for her sister so I wanted to warn you before they both get away."

Perun threw his head back and laughed. "So, this isn't about helping me, but getting your plaything back." He walked into the study off the foyer and poured himself a whiskey. He threw it back in one gulp.

Thane followed him into the room but stayed by the door. He didn't trust the mage.

"It's not just about power to you. I see how you look at her." Perun poured another inch in his glass. "You'd better watch yourself with that one. You'll end up dead. The curse is real."

"I can take care of myself." Thane backed out of the room, keeping Perun in his view.

"You never had any intention to tell me about this loophole. You only came to see if she was here." Perun narrowed his gaze at Thane.

Thane shrugged one shoulder and walked toward the front door. "Let me know if you see Jerina."

Thane hoped he gave Kosa enough time to switch boxes. He couldn't stay any longer or Perun would suspect something was up.

He took his time walking across the street and let the shadows close around him.

Jerina was waiting for him just up the road behind a large bush. He knew she had been watching the door to Perun's. He could feel her eyes on him.

As soon as he cleared the streetlight and stepped behind the bush, Jerina's arms wound around his neck.

"I was so worried!" She hugged him tightly, her chest aching with fear for him. "Do you think he suspected anything?"

Thane squeezed her to him. "No. Not at all. He was more concerned with me losing you than anything."

He left out the part about the curse. Jerina was worried enough about it. He didn't need to add that Perun was convinced that it was real.

"How long do you think it will take Kosa to sneak out?" Jerina wanted to storm inside and get her sister, but she knew they would have a better chance if Kosa came out on her own.

Twenty excruciatingly long minutes later, they spotted Kosa at the window of her bedroom. She slid the panes up and leaned out. She was holding something in her hands.

Jerina squinted to see what she was doing. Kosa struck a match and was placing it over the open pocket watch. As soon as the fire touched the watch, a horrifying scream shook the night. It sounded like the watch was being burnt alive.

Thane and Jerina ran toward the house. Kosa held the screaming watch helplessly, not knowing what to do. They had not anticipated the watch being a trap.

Kosa leaned out of the window. "The spell allowed me to take the watch, but I can't destroy it."

Lights flickered on through the house. Thane knew they had to get Kosa out of there immediately. "Throw it down to me. I'll burn it, while you climb down the ivy!"

Kosa tossed the watch to Thane.

"I can't leave the house until it is destroyed!"

The watch stopped screaming when Kosa dropped it, but once Thane created fire magic, it began to screech again. Thane intensified the fire, but it resisted.

They were running out of time. Jerina joined Thane and added her magic to his, making the fire roar with strength. The watch's back compartment opened, and the hair went up in flames quickly.

Kosa leaned out of the window, trying to force herself to climb out, but unable to do so. Once the hair began to sizzle, she felt the invisible barrier break, and she was able to slip from the room.

She reached the ground at the same time Perun flew out the front door with a gun in his hand.

"What have you done?" Perun demanded. He pointed the gun at Jerina. "You have been nothing but a problem to me since you first entered this town!" Perun stalked toward them, closing the space.

Jerina clenched her fists. "You will not control another vila. Ever!"

She took her sister's hand and backed up a few steps. They needed to get away from Perun. He was looking a little unhinged.

"You lost, Perun. Give up. No one should be enslaved by

another." Thane wanted to direct Perun's rage at him and not the girls. He needed to get them to safety and away from the gun.

"She is MINE! She belongs to ME!" Perun bellowed into the night.

Jerina stepped back again, but Perun followed. She didn't know how to get away from him while he was waving that gun. She had heard that guns didn't work well in Havenwood Falls and especially around supernaturals, so she was surprised he had one. The vila never used guns. They would not work correctly around all their magic.

"Kosa! You get back here right now! You are mine! MINE! You'll always be mine! I'll find you no matter where you go. I *will* find you. You'll never escape me."

Thane glanced at Jerina and Kosa. "I'll distract him. You two run for help."

Jerina shook her head. "I'm not leaving you. We're in this together."

"I'll be fine. Just go!" Thane needed them out of the way. He threw magic at Perun, but the mage was good enough with spells that he blasted it away from him.

Thane tried a stunning spell, but that too was reflected. His swords were not a match for a gun, so he needed to keep Perun talking and hopefully push him over the edge to do something stupid. "You're not man enough for a vila."

Jerina's jaw dropped. "What are you doing?"

Thane ignored her. "Yeah. The vila warrior couldn't wait to get away from you. And look where she ran. Straight to me."

Perun swung the gun toward Thane. "You're trying to steal them both for yourself! I won't let you get away with that."

Thane turned to glance at Jerina. "Run!" he mouthed.

Jerina was terrified for Thane. He had just turned the monster's attention solely on him. She needed to do something.

"You're nothing, Perun! You had to steal my sister to be a stronger mage. You didn't have enough power on your own to compete in your coven, so you decided to steal Kosa's," Jerina taunted. "You're a fool!"

Perun screamed inhumanly and flipped the gun toward Jerina. When he saw her smile, he pulled the trigger with a sneer. A deafening blast shook the street as the gun fired. Jerina's eyes grew huge as she saw the bullet head directly toward her.

Seconds before it was to hit her chest, Thane jumped in front of her and was shot in the chest.

"NOOOOOOO!" Jerina screamed in agony, her arms going around Thane as he fell to the ground. Red was spreading from the middle of his chest, soaking through his clothing.

Manic laughter filled the street after Jerina's scream ended.

"I win." Perun moved closer but was suddenly surrounded by members of the Court, who took him into custody.

Jerina ripped open Thane's shirt and gasped. The hole was huge and was rhythmically expelling blood. He was shot through the heart.

Jerina's hands began to shake as she tried to heal him, sending every ounce of power she had into him. His skin was closing up, but it didn't seem to be enough.

Thane lifted his hand to Jerina's tear-stricken face. "It's not going to work. The bullet was made of iron."

"No! No! It has to work. I won't let you die." Jerina sobbed as she continued to try to heal him.

Thane's grip was growing weaker. "It's okay. You're safe. He won't hurt you or Kosa again."

"Don't you dare give up, Thane! I won't let you!" Jerina gripped the edges of his shirt.

Thane smiled sadly. "I guess you were right. The curse is real. I love you."

"I love you too," Jerina sobbed, and then Thane's heart stopped beating.

Jerina's scream of outrage could be heard throughout Havenwood Falls. She unleashed her emotions all at once, creating a storm unlike ever before. Hurricane-force winds ripped through the valley. Thunder shook the houses, and lightning lit up the sky. Rain pelted down on the street, drenching anyone brave enough not to take cover.

Kosa sobbed as she watched her sister hold the man she loved. Damn the curse! She hated being a vila.

She watched her sister look up at the sky and knew she was asking the gods why they would do this to her.

Lightning struck a tree near where they were, throwing sparks into the air. The flash drew her attention and gave her an idea. Kosa let her power surge through her and reach for the storm. She didn't know if it would work, but it was worth a try.

Kosa connected with a bolt of lightning and guided it toward Thane, striking him in the chest.

Jerina's head whipped toward Kosa. "What are you doing to him?"

She lay across his chest, protecting him from everything, sobbing his name.

She felt him twitch, making her sit up and stare at his beautiful face, wondering if it was her imagination. Just then, he inhaled deeply and began to cough. The storm died down, and Jerina pulled her power back.

Kosa was at their side in an instant, her healing powers running through her hands. Jerina snapped out of her shock and joined her sister, locking their hands together.

After a moment, Thane opened his eyes and focused on Jerina.

She threw herself into his arms and kissed him hard. "Don't ever do that to me again!" She cried and laughed at the same time.

Thane hugged her to him. "We changed fate. You're stuck with me now."

Jerina pulled back so she could face him. "Forever?"

"Forever."

EPILOGUE

ne Week Later

The roar of the rushing water didn't drown out Jerina's thoughts, but she had hoped they would. She had too much on her mind and no idea what to do about it all.

She stared out at the falls, hoping answers would suddenly manifest. All that had appeared were four pixies playing in the underbrush near the falls. They seemed a little skittish, so she didn't try to speak with them.

Perun had been held in the basement of the courthouse in a magical cell that kept him from escaping until the Court of the Sun and the Moon decided his fate. It took them the entire week to deliberate before they finally decided that he would be banished from Havenwood Falls for fifty-five years.

Jerina had no idea how they came up with fifty-five years, but at least the residents of the town wouldn't have to worry about him for a long time. Warning her vila sisters to be on the lookout for him would be vital. She had a feeling he would be relentless in an attempt to seek revenge on her and Kosa.

She began planning everything they would need to do to prepare. Some camouflage around their village would have to be put in place so that he would never be able to find it again.

"Ugh," she muttered to herself.

She had responsibilities to her vila, but she knew her heart would remain in Havenwood Falls. It would be so easy to make a life with Thane. They loved each other, and they changed fate. That meant everything.

"I knew you would be here," Kosa called out as she approached her sister Jerina. A light breeze ruffled her blond hair.

Jerina pulled her focus from the falls and greeted Kosa with a big smile. "I love it here. There's so much magic in the falls and around this area. It—"

"Almost feels like home?" Kosa finished for her. She sat on the flat boulder next to Jerina, bumping her shoulder purposely.

Jerina nodded. "Yes. It does."

It was spring in Colorado, but the air around the falls was chilly, causing her to tug her jacket tighter.

The sisters sat quietly, each lost in their own thoughts as they gazed at the rushing water. Jerina watched a few fish jump from the waves, splashing down and disappearing from view.

Kosa took a deep fortifying breath. She couldn't delay any longer. "I'm not going back."

Jerina continued to stare into the falls.

"Did you hear what I said? I'm not returning." Kosa twisted to face Jerina.

Jerina blinked slowly and shifted around to her beloved sister. "I know." Grasping Kosa's hand, Jerina gently squeezed and then released Kosa. "I knew you would want to remain here." She paused. "Things will never be the same."

Kosa's shoulders dropped. "You're going back?"

Jerina slipped off the large rock and stepped toward the bank of the river. "I'm the leader of the warriors, and I must protect every vila. I can't abandon our sisters."

Kosa stormed over to Jerina. "You aren't an elder. You don't rule over the vila. Think about yourself for once."

"Who would train the warriors? How could we both leave?" Jerina pulled at her hair. Their mother would be furious, and not because she would miss her daughters. She would be afraid of the scandal and how it would affect her.

Kosa put her arm around Jerina's shoulders. "There are many who could, and would want to, step into your role as leader of the warriors."

Jerina crossed her arms over her chest and hugged herself. "Yes, but I need to make sure everyone is safe before I could even consider anything else."

Kosa tried to control the quaking in her legs at the thought of Perun out in the world somewhere. "We are safer from him here."

"Yes, we are, but our vila sisters need to be as well." Jerina wanted to stay, but didn't know how it could possibly work.

"It wouldn't take much to make them safe." Kosa loved the vila. But she needed this, and she knew Jerina did too. "What about Thane?"

"What about him?" Jerina shifted, suddenly uncomfortable.

"I know you love him." Kosa raised an eyebrow. "Don't try to deny it. Don't you want to stay here and see what happens with him? You love him, do you not?"

Jerina sighed. "It's not that simple."

"Yes. Yes, it is." Kosa bounced on her toes. "Has he asked you to stay?"

"She hasn't given me an answer yet." Thane strolled out of the woods and into the clearing by the waterfall.

Jerina's breath caught as she watched him move closer, his muscles rippling with each step.

Thane nodded at Kosa but continued to focus on Jerina. "I'm still waiting." He stepped into her space, crowding her, but she didn't seem to mind. He heard her breath catch and couldn't prevent a dazzling smile from brightening his face. "I came up with a solution."

Jerina had to clear her throat to answer him. "A solution to what?"

Kosa crossed her fingers and moved back to give them some privacy.

Thane leaned closer. "To everything. I know you don't have much in today's currency because the vila don't need it, so living independently here would be extremely difficult. You wouldn't be happy staying with my parents or at the inn and letting me pay for it."

Jerina frowned and retreated a step. "I already know all this."

Thane followed after her. "You didn't let me finish. I've been thinking about this a lot." He rubbed his hand down her arm, causing her to shiver. "There is a human gentleman who is getting ready to retire. He doesn't have any family to leave his business to and doesn't need any money. He wants his business to continue, but doesn't have anyone to take it over. I spoke with him, and he would love to take on two lovely exchange students who wanted to stay in Havenwood Falls and not return to their war-torn country."

Kosa couldn't pretend to give them a private moment any longer. "Really? What business?"

Thane didn't take his eyes off Jerina, but answered Kosa. "Mr. Scoop remembered how much you love his sundaes. He's looking forward to showing you how to make them."

Jerina's eyes lit up. "Charms Soda Shoppe?"

Thane grinned. "Yes. Perfect, isn't it?"

Jerina threw herself into his arms and hugged him tightly.

Thane crushed her to him. "Does this mean you're staying?"

Jerina pulled back a little and looked over at her sister. "What do you think?"

Kosa grinned widely. "I think we need to make sure you leave some ice cream for our customers."

Jerina rushed to her sister, and they embraced, laughing.

Kosa squeezed Jerina and stepped back. "I'll see you two in a little while at the inn. Madame Luiza is going to show me how to make cookies."

Thane watched the sisters' joy and knew that they were going to end up very happy in Havenwood Falls.

"Thank you so much for arranging this." Jerina would have to make a short trip back to the vila village, but it would no longer be her home.

Thane brushed hair out of her face. "I would do anything for you."

"I would do anything for you, too." Jerina's eyes twinkled and became a little watery. She'd never felt that way about anyone before. "I love you."

"Good. You're going to have to love me for a really long time, because I'm not letting you go." Thane slid his hands into her hair and sealed his vow with a toe-curling kiss.

We hope you enjoyed this story in the Legends of Havenwood Falls series featuring a variety of supernatural creatures. The series is a collaborative effort by multiple authors.

Books in the historical Legends of Havenwood Falls series:

Lost in Time by Tish Thawer
Dawn of the Witch Hunters by Morgan Wylie
Redemption's End by Eric R. Asher
Trapped Within a Wish by Brynn Myers
Blood and Damnation by Belinda Boring
Fated Beginnings by E.J. Fechenda
Emeline by Katie M. John
Released From a Curse by Brynn Myers
A Pack of Lies by Kallie Ross
Kiss the Ashes by Desiree Lafawn
Hidden Truths by Colleen Nye
Wrath and Retribution by Belinda Boring
Changing Fate by Char Webster

Rise of the Witch Hunters by Morgan Wylie
The Drowning Bride by Seven Jane

Also try the main Havenwood Falls series; the YA line, Havenwood Falls High; the darker, sexier side of town, Havenwood Falls Sin & Silk; and the local supernatural college, Sun & Moon Academy.

Stay up to date at www.HavenwoodFalls.com

Subscribe to our reader group and receive free stories and more!

ABOUT THE AUTHOR

Char Webster weaves suspense, mystery, romance, and humor into all of her books. She strives to make the paranormal world fit perfectly into real life, where anything seems to be possible.

Reading and getting lost in a story have always been Char Webster's favorite things to do. She has also had a love for writing, which led her to her daytime career in public relations and marketing. After years of writing for others, Char decided to write something for herself.

Her writing fulfills a lifelong dream of creating a world where people can escape reality for a little while. Char Webster adores living in South Jersey because she feels like it is in the center of everything. She loves pizza, hot sauce, French fries, dancing, photography, and trying new things.

Stay in touch with Char:
Facebook: www.facebook.com/CharWebsterAuthor
Twitter: www.twitter.com/JustaGirlinSJ
Instagram: www.Instragram.com/Char.Webster
Website: www.CharWebsterAuthor.com

ACKNOWLEDGMENTS

It's an honor to be a part of the Havenwood Falls family, and I am so very thankful to Kristie Cook for bringing me into her incredible shared world. There are so many talented authors who have contributed to Havenwood Falls, and I get to be one of them. A special thank you to Kristie Cook, Kallie Ross, Brynn Myers, Randi Cooley Wilson, and Amy Hale for allowing me to include their awesome characters in my story. It was so much fun to include them.

I love the cover to *Changing Fate*, so I definitely need to give a big thank you to Regina Wamba at Mae I Design for creating great covers for this universe.

A HUGE thank you to all family for all their support and love and putting up with my crazy writing schedule.

I want to send lots of love to all of the readers out there. You are amazing. Thank you all for reading my books and showing me so much love. I also want to give a very big thank you to the Havenwood Falls Book Club and to Char's Gifted Society for being awesome and supporting me and my books.

AN EXCERPT

A Legends of Havenwood Falls Novella

HAVENWOOD FALLS LEGENDS

RISE OF THE WITCH HUNTERS

USA TODAY BESTSELLING AUTHOR

MORGAN WYLIE

This sequel to *Dawn of the Witch Hunters* by *USA Today* bestselling author Morgan Wylie continues the story of Marie and Judson.

Marie Blackstone is settling into her new life with Judson Carter in the beautiful box canyon they now call home. On a constant quest to prove her legitimacy—especially to the witches—Marie goes to great lengths to follow a feeling she's only encountered once before and hoped never to again. Someone's practicing the dark arts, but she can't quite discern who.

Within their growing settlement, darkness has found its way through the town's protective wards. And it seems to have an insatiable thirst for magic—witch magic. When witches begin to disappear or turn up drained of their magic, suspicion and fear grow. And some are looking at Marie, the resident witch hunter.

Finding her powers inconsistent and unreliable, Marie struggles to believe in herself and trust her abilities, especially as members of the town begin to doubt her. If she can't find and destroy the black magic and save the witches, she could lose the life she fought so hard to find—and ultimately her soul.

RISE OF THE WITCH HUNTERS

BY MORGAN WYLIE

1858 WHISPER FALLS

Marie Blackstone meandered down an aisle, passing through new shoots of grape vines in the oldest section of the Blackstone vineyard. The aroma of the sticky sweet fruit wafted into her nose as she passed by. As she approached the large outbuilding, she expected to run into the waiting arms of her husband, Judson. Except he wasn't standing with the barrels of wine where he was supposed to be. Noting her bare feet, Marie paused and slowly turned her head, realizing she was not alone. She took in the faces of a small crowd of townspeople around her, but something strange happened. Faces distorted and blurred. Her pulse quickened, and she looked around with panic.

Where's Judson?

Beyond the blurred faces, trees slowly enclosed around them. Within the trees, Marie spotted something—something she couldn't quite define. Dark wispy shadows of swirling masses wrapped around the trees, moving closer, stretching out tendrils of smoke, and invading the town and the people within it. Marie doubled over. Her stomach hurt so bad with the effects of dark magic she thought she would be sick. Her hands shook. Her head swam with visions of darkness, and dizziness took her down to her knees.

Judson! Where are you? Marie screamed but no sound came from her mouth. Her words were trapped in her mind.

Soon the townspeople faded from her view, consumed by the darkness as it moved closer toward her. Silhouettes emerged but not enough to recognize who or what they were. Were they supernatural? Were they creatures of some kind? Were they the souls of people she knew?

Out of nowhere Judson shot out in front of Marie, holding some kind of tool—a small sword with a glowing stone, her family dagger —sending a jolt of light toward the darkness. The light mixed with the power Judson had somehow infused it with and pushed the darkness back with hisses of displeasure screeching through the night.

Judson! Judson! Marie called again, but she couldn't seem to reach him with her voice. Instead she reached out her hand to grab his, but he, too, faded away from her with the townspeople. Marie heard words before she also faded into nothingness:

"Release me, Marie."

Then darkness swallowed her.

Marie awoke gasping for air, doubled over in pain. Her brow was slicked with sweat as she opened her eyes and took in the room around her. She pushed back her long blond hair away from her sticky skin. Home. She was in her bed.

A dream. It had all been a dream. Then why did she still feel so sick? Could it also be a warning?

Marie wasn't surprised to not see Judson in bed next to her. Since they'd been married, he'd been busy with blacksmith work. She called out, her voice dry and scratchy from sleep, "Judson? Are you there?"

When Judson didn't reply, she stumbled to her feet and went in search of him. The more she moved, the more she felt herself coming back from the brink of whatever ailment she had experienced. Her heart rate slowed to normal, and her breathing finally caught up with her. She had only felt a feeling so strong once before, when she and Judson had traveled across the country by wagon train with the other original settlers. They had stumbled upon an encampment of witches—witches who had been performing black magic. Unfortunately, her brother Dante and his band of rogue witch hunters had killed them all before she arrived and had the chance to stop him. He had been sending her a message: *This is our calling. This is our destiny: to rid the earth of all those capable of destructive magic.* However, Marie knew he wouldn't stop at users of dark magic alone. No, he would kill any and all witches if he could. He felt it was their birthright.

Marie felt differently.

She wanted to find a way to coexist. She had friends who were witches, and her mother had found peace among them before she died. Marie chose to follow in her mother's footsteps. Plus, she wouldn't have Judson if she went along with the idea of who they thought a witch hunter should be. Judson may not have been a witch, but he was raised by one within an entire coven of witches. So to Dante, Judson was just as evil.

Marie paused in front of an open window and gazed out at their beautiful new surroundings they called home—well, not so new, considering they had been living in the quaint box canyon area for a few years now. The sight of the mountains boxing them in on all four sides still warmed her heart and freely offered her peace, especially when a fresh thin layer of snow had fallen overnight, as it had the past night. Snow was early for September but not unheard of in the mountains. It wouldn't last through the day, however. The sun had just barely begun to make its ascent into the sky, but soft pink still welcomed the coming day.

Marie smiled when she noticed man-sized footprints traveling away from their home toward the shed Judson had set up as a blacksmith's forge. He had earned quite the reputation for his metalwork around town, and he'd been attempting to catch up on orders he had yet to fulfill. She had no doubt that was where he'd been since before dawn, working his heart out. Judson's personal metalwork took a back seat while he worked on orders for the townspeople, early in the morning or late into the evening, to make ends meet.

Marie dressed for the cold winds of fall she was about to face and wrapped herself with a heavy shawl. Theirs was a modest home built right next to the land they had claimed for the vineyard they were cultivating with such love and devotion. The house had just enough rooms for the family who had traveled with them: Marie's human father Hank, her human brother Rodney, her young adult hunter cousins Caroline and Michael, as well as a few other cousins who never fully awakened into their hunter side. Also, Rachael Stronghold—Marie's best friend from the coven Judson was raised in—and Ahote Ahusaka traveled and lived with them. Rachael and Ahote were now married with an emerging toddler named Alo Stronghold Ahusaka, after Ahote's brother and Rachael's maiden name for her mother who died before they had arrived. Needless to say, they were living in tight quarters.

Marie dreamed of one day being able to add additional rooms—perhaps even additional little cabins—to their home not only for family but for visitors who came to the area. The view was magnificent, and she wanted to share the peace and comfort she had found there with others. Then when the vineyard was fully functional and they had enough workers to sustain it, Marie dreamed of a larger, grander home closer to the falls to live out her days with Judson, hopefully raising a family of their own.

For the last several years since arriving in town, the original settlers had begun calling the area Whisper Falls due to the way the falls had beckoned them, whispering into their souls, to come. And when they stood in the center of the little canyon, the falls sounded like a whisper, and so they had begun to build the town in that very spot. However, other names had been bandied about —many wanted to include *haven* in the name, since that was the purpose of the town—and there was still much discussion about it.

As she exited the warm and cozy home—thanks to one of the early risers' forethought to build a fire—she inhaled slow and deep, feeling the sharp sting of the bitterly cold air as it flooded her lungs, and smiled. Though jarring, the feeling reminded her she was alive. She loved fall in the little box canyon. It wasn't unheard of to find snow this early; still, she proceeded with caution as she made her way toward the forge. Marie carefully avoided patches of ice and areas of thicker frost. Loving the squeaking sound her boots made against the snow, Marie paused to listen for the whispers from the falls. This time of morning, the town was quiet and the rushing water could clearly be heard. She closed her eyes and could practically feel the mist spray off the water and onto her face. Such a great sense of importance, of magic, and of purpose she felt next to the waters.

The memory instantly took her back to when they had first arrived. She and Judson had picnicked by the edge of the lower pool. She had just discovered that the stone set into the dagger Judson had given her had immense power when it touched the magical waters, but when it was interlocked with her ancestor's journal, the pages within had revealed much more about who she was as a Blackstone than she had ever known. The secrets and knowledge she had been seeking since her mother died had finally been revealed. It was also then and in that space, Judson Carter proposed to her—again. His action was not necessary, as they had been married in secret back in Virginia before they left, but he wanted to make a symbolic statement of their new life. Shortly after they established their life in the mountains and secured their position, they had asked Raffaele Augustine to marry them again. She wanted friends, not just strangers, to witness their union. And it had taken them some time and experience to gain that trust and companionship she had so longed for.

Purchase *Rise of the Witch Hunters* where books are sold.